DUBLIN PEOPLE

SHORT STORIES

Do you ever stare at strangers on a bus or a train, and wonder who they are and what they're like? A girl, going home from her job to an empty bedsitter, perhaps. She looks shy, unsure of herself, probably doesn't find it easy to make friends . . .

Or a middle-aged man, with a cheerful sort of face – the kind of man who likes to have a drink and a joke in the pub with his friends. But now he looks irritable, depressed, maybe even a little guilty . . .

Here, in short stories full of compassion and humour, Maeve Binchy takes us into the lives of two such people. Irish people, living in Dublin, but we would recognize them anywhere. Jo, newly come to the big city . . . and Gerry, a man with a problem. We share their anxieties and hopes, their foolishness, even their tragedy . . .

INSTITUTE FOR APPLIED LANGUAGE STUDIES
UNIVERSITY OF EDIN...

E

D1149982

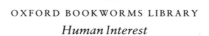

OXFORD BOOKWORMS LIBRARY

Human Interest

Dublin People

SHORT STORIES

Stage 6 (2500 headwords)

Series Editor: Jennifer Bassett
Founder Editor: Tricia Hedge
Activities Editors: Jennifer Bassett and Alison Baxter

MAEVE BINCHY

Dublin People

SHORT STORIES

Retold by
Jennifer Bassett

OXFORD UNIVERSITY PRESS

OXFORD
UNIVERSITY PRESS

Great Clarendon Street, Oxford OX2 6DP

Oxford University Press is a department of the University of Oxford.
It furthers the University's objective of excellence in research, scholarship,
and education by publishing worldwide in

Oxford New York

Auckland Bangkok Buenos Aires Cape Town Chennai
Dar es Salaam Delhi Hong Kong Istanbul Karachi Kolkata
Kuala Lumpur Madrid Melbourne Mexico City Mumbai
Nairobi São Paulo Shanghai Taipei Tokyo Toronto

OXFORD and OXFORD ENGLISH are registered trade marks of
Oxford University Press in the UK and in certain other countries

Original edition © Maeve Binchy 1982
First published by Ward River Press Ltd, Eire 1982
This simplified edition © Oxford University Press 2000

The moral rights of the author have been asserted

Database right Oxford University Press (maker)

First published in Oxford Bookworms 1993
4 6 8 10 12 13 11 9 7 5

No unauthorized photocopying

All rights reserved. No part of this publication may be reproduced,
stored in a retrieval system, or transmitted, in any form or by any means,
without the prior permission in writing of Oxford University Press,
or as expressly permitted by law, or under terms agreed with the appropriate
reprographics rights organization. Enquiries concerning reproduction
outside the scope of the above should be sent to the ELT Rights Department,
Oxford University Press, at the address above

You must not circulate this book in any other binding or cover
and you must impose this same condition on any acquirer

Any websites referred to in this publication are in the public domain and
their addresses are provided by Oxford University Press for information only.
Oxford University Press disclaims any responsibility for the content

ISBN 0 19 423084 8

Printed in Spain by Unigraf S.L.

Illustrated by: Susan Sluglett

The publishers have made every effort to contact the copyright holder of
the painting reproduced on the cover of this title, but have been unable to do so.
If the copyright holder would like to contact the publishers, the publishers
would be happy to pay an appropriate reproduction fee

The two stories in this volume appeared in their original form in the
collection of short stories by Maeve Binchy entitled *Dublin 4*

CONTENTS

FLAT IN RINGSEND

Jo knew what she should do. She should get the evening papers at lunch-time, read all the advertisements for flats, and as soon as she saw one that looked suitable, she should rush round at once and sit on the doorstep. Never mind if the advertisement said 'After six o'clock'. She knew that if she went at six o'clock, and the flat was a good one, she'd probably find a queue of people all down the street. Finding a good flat in Dublin, at a rent you could afford, was like finding gold in the gold rush.

The other way was by personal contact. If you knew someone who knew someone who was leaving a flat . . . That was often a good way. But for somebody who had only just arrived in Dublin, there was no chance of any personal contact. No, it was a matter of staying in a hostel and searching.

Jo had been to Dublin several times when she was a child. She had been on school excursions, and to visit Dad that time he had been in hospital and everyone had been crying in case he wouldn't get better. Most of her friends, though, had been up to Dublin much more often. They talked in a familiar way about places they had gone to, and they assumed that Jo knew what they were talking about.

'You *must* know the Dandelion Market. Let me see, you

1

come out of the Zhivago and you go in a straight line to your right, keep going and you pass O'Donoghues and the whole of Stephen's Green, and you don't turn right down Grafton Street. Now do you know where it is?'

After such a long, helpful explanation, Jo said that she did know. Jo was always anxious to please other people, and she felt that she only annoyed them by not knowing what they were talking about. But really she knew hardly anything about Dublin. She felt that she was stepping into an unknown world when she got on the train to go and work there. She hadn't asked herself why she was going. Everyone had assumed that she would go. Who would stay in a one-horse town, the end of the world, this dead-and-alive place? At school all the girls were going to get out, escape, do some real living. Some of Jo's class had gone as far as Ennis or Limerick, often to stay with cousins. A few had gone to England, where an older sister or an aunt would help them to start a new life. But only Jo was going to Dublin, and she had no relations there. She was going off on her own.

There had been a lot of jokes about her going to work in the Post Office. There'd be no trouble in getting a stamp to write a letter home; what's more, there'd be no excuse if she didn't. She could make the occasional secret free phone call, too . . . which would be fine, except that her family didn't have a phone at home. Maybe she could send a ten-page telegram if she needed to say anything in a hurry. People assumed that she would soon know everything about people's private business in Dublin, in the same way as Miss Hayes knew everyone's business from the post office at home. They said that she'd find it very easy to get to know people. There was nowhere like a post office for making friends; it was the centre of everything.

Jo knew that she would be working in a small local post office, but her dreams of life in Dublin had been about the big General Post Office in the centre. She had imagined herself working there, chatting up all the customers as they came in, and knowing every single person who came to buy stamps or collect the children's allowances. She had dreamt of living somewhere nearby, in the heart of the city, maybe on the corner of O'Connell Bridge, so that she could look at the Liffey river from her bedroom.

She had never expected the miles and miles of streets where nobody knew anyone, the endless bus journeys, and setting off for work very early in the morning in case she got lost or the bus was cancelled.

'Not much time for a social life,' she wrote home. 'I'm so exhausted when I get back to the hostel that I just go to bed and fall asleep.'

Jo's mother thought it would be great if Jo stayed permanently in the girls' hostel. It was run by nuns, and Jo could come to no harm there. Her father said that he hoped they kept the place warm; nuns were famous for freezing everyone else to death just because they themselves wore very warm underclothes. Jo's sisters, who worked in the local hotel as waitresses, said Jo must be mad to have stayed a whole week in a hostel. Her brother who worked in the market said he was sorry she didn't have a flat; it would be somewhere to stay whenever he went to Dublin. Her brother who worked in the garage said that Jo should have stayed at home. What was the point of going to live in Dublin? Jo would only get discontented and become like that O'Hara girl, happy neither in Dublin nor at home. However, everybody knew that he had been keen on the O'Hara girl for a long time, and was very annoyed that she wouldn't stay quietly in her home town and be like a normal woman.

But Jo didn't know that they were all thinking about her and discussing her, as she answered the advertisement for the flat in Ringsend. It said, *Own room, own television, share kitchen, bathroom.* It was very near her post office and seemed too good to be true. Please, God, please. I hope it's nice, I hope they like me, I hope it's not too expensive.

There wasn't a queue for this one because it wasn't really a flat to rent; the advertisement had said, *Third girl wanted.* Jo wondered if 'own television' meant that the place was too expensive or too high-class for her, but the house did not look very frightening. It was in a row of ordinary, red-brick houses with basements. Her father had warned her against basements; they were full of damp, he said, but then her father had a bad chest and saw damp everywhere. But the flat was not in the basement, it was upstairs. And a cheerful-looking girl wearing a university scarf, obviously a failed applicant, was coming down the stairs.

'Dreadful place,' she said to Jo. 'The girls are both awful. As common as dirt.'

'Oh,' said Jo and went on climbing.

'Hallo,' said the girl with 'Nessa' printed on her T-shirt. 'God, did you see that awful upper-class cow going out? I just can't put up with that kind of girl, I really hate them . . .'

'What did she do?' asked Jo.

'Do? She didn't have to *do* anything. She just looked around and wrinkled her lip and gave a rude little laugh, and then said, "Is this it? Oh dear, oh dear," in her silly upper-class accent.

4

Stupid old cow. We wouldn't have had her in here even if we were starving and needed her rent to buy a piece of bread . . . would we, Pauline?'

Pauline was wearing a shirt of such blindingly bright colours that it hurt the eyes to look at it. But the colour of her hair was almost as bright as her shirt. Pauline was a punk, Jo noted with amazement. She had seen punks on O'Connell Street, but she had never talked to one.

'No, stupid old bore,' said Pauline. 'That girl was such a bore. She'd have bored us to death. Years later our bodies would have been found here and the judge would have said that it was death by boredom . . .'

Jo laughed. It was such a wild thought to think of all that pink hair, lying dead on the floor, because it had been bored to death by an upper-class accent.

'I'm Jo,' she began, 'I work in the post office and I rang . . .'

Nessa said they were just about to have a mug of tea. She brought out three mugs; one had 'Nessa', one had 'Pauline', and the last one had 'Other' written on it. 'We'll get your name put on if you come to stay,' Nessa said generously.

Both girls had office jobs nearby. They had got the flat three months ago and Nessa's sister had had the third room, but now she was getting married very quickly, very quickly indeed, and so the room was empty. They explained the cost, they showed Jo the hot-water heater in the bathroom, and they showed her the cupboard in the kitchen, each shelf with a name on it – Nessa, Pauline, and Maura.

'Maura's name will go, and we'll paint in yours if you come to stay,' Nessa said again, in a friendly way.

'You've no sitting room,' Jo said.

'No, we made the flat into three <u>bedsitters,</u>' said Nessa.

'Makes much more sense,' said Pauline.

'What's the point of a sitting room?' asked Nessa.

'I mean, who's going to sit in it?' asked Pauline.

'And we've got two chairs in our own rooms,' Nessa said proudly.

'And each of us has our own television,' said Pauline happily.

That was the point that Jo wanted to discuss.

'Yes, you didn't say how much that costs. Do I have to pay rent for the TV?'

There was a wide smile on Nessa's big happy face. 'Not a penny. You see, Maura's boyfriend, Steve, well, her husband now, I hope; anyway, Steve worked in the business and he was able to get us TVs for almost nothing.'

'So you bought them – you don't rent them at all?' Jo was delighted.

'Well, bought . . . in a manner of speaking,' Pauline said. 'We certainly accepted them.'

'Yeah, it was Steve's way of saying thank you, his way of paying the rent . . . in a manner of speaking,' Nessa said.

'But did he stay here too?'

'He was Maura's boyfriend. He stayed most of the time.'

'Oh,' said Jo. There was a silence.

'Well?' Nessa said accusingly. 'If you've got anything to say, you should say it now.'

'I suppose I was wondering . . . didn't he get in everyone's way? I mean, if a fourth person was staying in the flat, was it fair on the others?'

'Why do you think we organized the flat into bedsits?' Pauline asked. 'It means we can all do what we like, when we like, without getting in each other's way. Right?'

'Right,' Nessa said.

'Right,' Jo said, doubtfully.

'So what do you think?' Nessa asked Pauline. 'I think Jo would be OK if she wants to come, don't you?'

'Yeah, sure, I think she'd be fine if she'd like it here,' said Pauline.

'Thank you,' said Jo, her face going a little pink.

'Is there anything else you'd like to ask? I think we've told you everything. There's a phone with a coin-box in the hall downstairs. There are three nurses in the flat below us, but they don't take any messages for us so we don't take any for them. The rent has to be paid on the first of the month, plus five pounds each, and I buy a few basics for the flat.'

'Will you come, then?' asked Nessa.

'Please. I'd like to very much. Can I come on Sunday night?'

They gave her a key, took her rent money, poured another mug of tea, and said that it was great to have fixed it all up so quickly. Nessa said that Jo was such a short name it would be really easy to paint it onto the shelf in the kitchen, the shelf in the bathroom and her mug.

'She wanted to paint the names on the doors too, but I wouldn't let her,' said Pauline.

'Pauline thought it would look too much like a children's nursery,' said Nessa regretfully.

'That's right,' laughed Pauline. 'I wanted to leave a bit of variety in life. If our names are on the doors, then we'll never get any surprise visitors during the night – and I always like a bit of the unexpected!'

Jo laughed too. She hoped they were joking.

7

*   *   *

Jo wrote to her mother and told her that the flat was in a very nice district. She told her father how far it was from the damp basement, and she mentioned the television in each bedroom in order to make her sisters jealous. They had said she was stupid to go to Dublin; the best Dublin people all came to County Clare on their holidays. Why didn't she stay at home and meet them there, rather than going to the city and trying to find them in their own place?

*   *   *

It was tea-time in the hostel on Sunday when Jo said goodbye. She struggled with her two suitcases to the bus stop.

'Your friends aren't going to collect you?' asked Sister Mary, one of the nuns.

'They haven't a car, Sister.'

'I see. Often, though, young people come to help a friend. I hope they are kind people, your friends.'

'Very kind, Sister.'

'That's good. Well, God be with you, child, and remember that this is a very wicked city. There's a lot of very wicked people in it.'

'Yes, Sister. I'll keep my eyes open for them.'

It took her a long time to get to the flat.

She had to change buses twice, and was nearly exhausted when she got there. She struggled up the stairs with her cases and into her new room. It was smaller than it had looked on Friday, but it could hardly have shrunk. On the bed were two blankets and two pillows, but no sheets. Oh God, she'd forgotten about sheets. And of course, there was no towel either. She'd assumed that they would be included. How stupid of her not to have asked.

She hoped the girls wouldn't notice, and that she'd be able to go out in her lunch hour tomorrow and buy some. At least she had her savings to use for just this kind of emergency.

She put away all her clothes in the narrow little cupboard, and put out her ornaments on the window sill and her shoes in a neat line on the floor. She put her suitcases under the bed and sat down, feeling very dull.

Back in her home town her friends would be going out to the cinema or to a Sunday night dance. In the hostel some of the girls would be watching television in the sitting room, others would have gone to the cinema together. Then they would buy fish and chips to eat on the way home, throwing the papers into the rubbish bin on the corner of the street because Sister didn't like the smell of chips coming into the building.

Not one of them was sitting alone on a bed with nothing to do. She could go out and take the bus into the centre and go to the cinema alone. But that seemed silly when she had her own television. Her very own. She could change to a different programme whenever she wanted to; she wouldn't have to ask anyone.

She was about to go to the sitting room to look for a Sunday newspaper, when she remembered there was no sitting room. She didn't want to open the doors of their rooms in case they came in and found her looking. She wondered where they were. Was Nessa out with a boyfriend? She hadn't mentioned one, but then girls in Dublin didn't tell you immediately if they had a boyfriend or not. Perhaps Pauline was at a punk disco. Jo couldn't believe that anyone would actually employ Pauline with that bright pink hair and let her meet the public, but maybe she was kept hidden in a back office. Surely the girls would be home by about eleven o'clock? Perhaps then they could all have a cup of hot chocolate together in the sitting room – well, in the kitchen, to end the day. Meanwhile, she would sit back and watch her very own television.

Jo fell asleep after half an hour. She had been very tired. She dreamed that Nessa and Pauline had come in. Pauline had decided to wash the pink out of her hair and share a room with Nessa. They were going to turn Pauline's room into a sitting room where they would sit and talk and plan. She woke up suddenly when she heard laughter. It was Pauline and a man's voice, and they had gone into the kitchen.

Jo shook herself. She must have been asleep for three hours; she had a stiff neck and the television was still going. She stood up and turned it off, combed her hair and was about to go out and welcome the homecomers when she hesitated. If Pauline had invited a boy home, perhaps she was going to take him to bed with her. Perhaps she wouldn't want her new flatmate coming out to join in the conversation. They were laughing in the kitchen, she could hear them, then she heard the kettle whistling. Ah, she could always pretend that she just wanted to make herself a cup of tea.

Nervously, she opened the door and went into the kitchen. Pauline was with a young man who wore a heavy leather jacket with a lot of bits of metal on it.

'Hallo, Pauline, I was just going to get myself a cup of tea,' Jo said apologetically.

'Sure,' Pauline said. She was not unfriendly, she didn't look annoyed, but she made no effort to introduce her friend.

Nervously, she opened the door and went into the kitchen.

The kettle was still hot so Jo found a mug with 'Visitor' on it and put in a tea bag.

'Nessa's going to paint my name on a mug,' she said to the man in the jacket, just for something to say.

'Oh, good,' he said. He looked at Pauline and asked, 'Who's Nessa?'

'Lives over there,' Pauline said, pointing in the direction of Nessa's room.

'I'm the third girl,' Jo said desperately.

'Third in what?' the man said, puzzled.

Pauline had finished making her tea and was moving towards the door, carrying two mugs.

'Goodnight,' she said cheerfully.

'Goodnight, Pauline, goodnight . . . er . . .' Jo said.

She took her mug of tea into her own room and turned on her television again. She turned it up quite loud in case she heard the sound of anything next door. She hoped she hadn't annoyed Pauline. She didn't think she had done anything to annoy her, and anyway Pauline had seemed cheerful enough when she was taking this boy off to – well, to her own room. Jo sighed and got into bed.

* * *

Next morning she was coming out of the bathroom when she met Nessa.

'Jo is just two letters, "J" and "O", isn't it?' Nessa asked.

'Oh yes, that's right, thank you very much, Nessa.'

'Right. I didn't want to paint your name and then find you had an "E" on it.'

'No, no, it's short for Josephine.'

'Right.' Nessa was already on her way out.

'What time are you coming home tonight?' Jo asked.

'Oh, I don't think I'll have done your name by tonight,' Nessa said.

'I didn't mean that. I just wondered what you were doing for your tea . . . supper. You know?'

'No idea,' said Nessa cheerfully.

'Oh,' said Jo. 'Sorry.'

*   *   *

Jacinta, who worked beside Jo in the post office, asked her how the flat was.

'It's great,' Jo said.

'You were right to get out of that hostel. You can't live your own life in a hostel,' Jacinta said wisely.

'No, no indeed.'

'God, I wish I didn't live at home,' Jacinta said. 'It's not natural for people to live with their own parents. There should be a law about it. There are laws about stupid things like not bringing living chickens into the country – who would want to do that anyway? – But there are no laws about the things that people really need.'

'Yes,' said Jo dutifully.

'Anyway, you'll be having a great time from now on. Country girls like you have all the luck.'

'I suppose we do,' Jo agreed doubtfully.

*   *   *

Jo bought a hamburger on the way home and ate it. She washed some underclothes, she put the new sheets on the bed and hung her new towel up in the bathroom. She took out her writing paper but remembered that she had written home on Friday just after she had found the flat. There was nothing new to tell.

If she had stayed in the hostel, they might have been playing a game of cards in the sitting room now. Or someone might have bought a new record. The girls would be looking at the evening paper, sighing over the price of flats, wondering whether to go to the cinema. There would be talk, and endless cups of tea or bottles of Coke from the machine. There would not be four walls as there were now.

The evening stretched emptily ahead of her. And then there would be Tuesday and Wednesday and Thursday . . . Tears came into her eyes and ran down her face as she sat on the end of her bed. She must be a really horrible person, she thought, to have no friends and nowhere to go and nothing to do. Other people of eighteen had a great time. She used to have a great time when she was seventeen, at school and planning to be eighteen. Look at her now, sitting alone. Even her flatmates didn't want to have anything to do with her. Jo cried and cried. Then she got a headache so she took two headache pills and climbed into bed. It's bloody fantastic being grown up, she thought, as she switched off the light at nine o'clock.

* * *

There was a 'J' on the place where her towel hung, her name was on the bathroom shelf that belonged to her, and her empty kitchen shelf had a 'Jo' on it also. She examined the other two shelves. Nessa had breakfast cereal and a packet of sugar and a lot of tins of soup on her shelf. Pauline had a biscuit tin and several tins of grapefruit on hers.

The kitchen was nice and tidy. Nessa had said the first day that they never left any washing up to be done and that if you used the frying pan, you had to clean it then, not leave it in the sink until the morning. It had all seemed great fun when she was talking about it then, because Jo had imagined midnight suppers, and all three of them laughing and having parties. That's what people *did*, for heaven's sake. She must have come to live with two really unsociable people, that was her problem.

Pauline came in to the kitchen yawning, and opened a tin of grapefruit.

'I think I'd never wake up if I didn't have this,' she said. 'I have half a tin of grapefruit and two biscuits for my breakfast every day, then I'm ready for anything.'

Jo was pleased to be spoken to.

'Is your friend here?' she said, trying to sound modern and up to date.

'Which friend?' Pauline yawned and began to spoon the grapefruit out of the tin into a bowl.

'You know, your friend, the other night?'

'Nessa?' Pauline looked at her, not understanding. 'Do you mean Nessa?'

'No, the fellow, the man with the leather jacket with the metal bits. I met him here in the kitchen.'

'Oh yes. Shane.'

'Shane. That was his name.'

'Yeah, what about him, what were you saying?'

'I was asking if he was here.'

'Here? Now? Why should he be here?' Pauline pushed her pink hair out of her eyes and looked at her watch. 'Jesus Christ, it's only twenty to eight in the morning. Why would he be here?'

15

She looked wildly around the kitchen as if the man with the leather jacket was going to appear from behind the gas cooker. Jo felt the conversation was going wrong.

'I just asked sociably if he was still here, that was all.'

'But why on earth would he be still here? I went out with him on Sunday night. *Sunday.* It's Tuesday morning now, isn't it? Why would he be here?' Pauline looked confused and worried, and Jo wished she had never spoken.

'I just thought he was your boyfriend . . .'

'No, he's not, but if he was, I tell you I wouldn't have him here at twenty to eight in the morning talking! I don't know how anyone can talk in the mornings. I just don't understand it.'

Jo drank her tea silently.

'See you,' said Pauline eventually when she had finished her grapefruit and biscuits, and crashed into the bathroom.

Jo thanked Nessa for putting up the names. Nessa was pleased.

'I like doing that. It gives me a sense of order in the world. It gives everything a place in the system, and that makes me feel better.'

'Sure,' said Jo. She was just about to ask Nessa what she was doing that evening when she remembered the lack of interest that Nessa had shown yesterday. She decided to express it differently this time.

'Are you off out with your friends this evening?' she said cautiously.

'I might be, I might not, it's always hard to know in the morning, isn't it?'

'Yes, it is,' said Jo untruthfully. It was becoming increasingly easy to know in the morning, she thought. The answer was coming up loud and clear when she asked herself what she was going to do in the evening. The answer was Nothing.

'Well, I'm off now. Goodbye,' she said to Nessa.

Nessa looked up and smiled. 'Bye bye,' she said absent-mindedly, as if Jo had been the postman or the man delivering milk on the street.

*   *   *

On Thursday night Jo went downstairs to answer the phone. It was for one of the nurses on the ground floor as it always was. She knocked quietly on their door. The big fair-haired nurse thanked her, and as Jo was going up the stairs again she heard the girl say, 'No, it was one of the people in the flats upstairs. There's three flats upstairs and we all share the same phone.'

That was it. That was what she hadn't realized. She wasn't in a flat with two other girls; she was in a flat by herself. Why hadn't she understood that? She was in a proper bedsitter all of her own; she just shared the kitchen and bathroom.

That's what had been wrong. She had thought that she was meant to be part of a friendly all-girls-together flat. That's why she had been so miserable. She thought back through the whole conversation with Nessa on the first day. She remembered what they had said about turning the flat into bedsitters but not telling the landlord anything – it was never a good idea to tell landlords anything, just keep paying the rent and keep out of his way.

There was quite a cheerful smile on her face now. I'm on my own in Dublin, she thought, I have my own place, I'm going out to find a life for myself now. She didn't have to worry about Pauline's behaviour any more now. If Pauline wanted to bring home a rough-looking person with metal bits on his jacket, that was Pauline's business. She just lived in the flat next door. That's what Pauline had meant when she had said Nessa lived next door. And that's why Nessa was so keen on all this labelling and naming things. No wonder they had been slightly surprised when she kept asking them what they were doing in the evening. They must have thought she was mad.

Happy for the first time since Sunday, Jo got herself ready for a night out. She put on eyeshadow and mascara, she put some colour on her cheeks and wore her big earrings. She didn't know where she was going, but she decided that she would go out cheerfully now. She looked around her room and liked it much better. She would get some pictures for the walls, she would even ask her mother if she could take some of the ornaments from home. The kitchen shelves at home were packed full with ornaments; her mother would be glad to give some of them a new home. Singing happily to herself, she set off.

She felt really great as she walked purposefully along the street. She pitied her sisters who were only now finishing their evening's work at the hotel. She pitied the girls who still had to stay in a hostel, who hadn't been able to go out and find a place of their own. She felt sorry for Jacinta who had to stay at home and whose mother and father questioned her about where she went and what she did. She pitied people who had to share televisions. What if you wanted to watch one programme and they wanted to watch something else? How did you decide? She was so full of cheerful thoughts that she nearly walked past the pub where the notice said: *Tonight – the Great Gaels.*

Imagine, the Great Gaels were there in person. In a pub. Entrance charge £1. If she paid a pound, she would see them close to. Up to now she had only seen them on television.

They had been at her local town once about four years ago, before they were famous. She remembered seeing an advertisement, saying that they would be in this pub tonight, and now here she was outside it.

Jo's heart beat fast. Was it a thing you could do on your own, go into a concert in a pub? Probably it was a thing that people went to in groups; she might look odd. Maybe there'd be no place for just one person to sit. Maybe it would only be tables for groups.

But then a great wave of courage came flooding over her. She was a young woman who lived in a flat on her own in Dublin, she had her own place and by the Lord, if she could do that, she could certainly go into a pub and hear the Great Gaels on her own. She pushed the door.

A man sat at the desk inside and gave her a ticket and took her pound.

'Where do I go?' she almost whispered.

'For what?' he asked.

'You know, where exactly do I go?' she asked. It seemed like an ordinary pub to her. There was no stage. Maybe the Great Gaels were upstairs.

The man assumed that she was looking for the toilet. 'I think the Ladies is over there near the other door, yes, there it is, beside the Gents.' He pointed across the room.

Her face turning a dark red, she thanked him. In case he was still looking at her, she thought she had better go to the Ladies. Inside, she looked at her face in the mirror. It had looked fine at home, back in her flat. In here it looked a bit dull, no character, no colour. The light wasn't very bright but she put on a lot more make-up, and then came out to find out where the concert would be held.

She saw two women sitting together. They looked safe enough to ask. They told her with a look of surprise that the concert would be in the pub, but not for about an hour.

'What do we do until then?' she asked.

They laughed. 'I suppose you could consider having a drink. It is a pub, after all,' said one of them. They went back to their conversation.

Jo felt very silly. She didn't want to leave and come back in case she had to buy another ticket to get in again. She wished she had brought a newspaper or a book. Everyone else seemed to be talking.

She sat for what seemed like a very long time. Twice the waiter asked her if she would like another drink as he cleaned the table around her glass of orange juice, which she was trying to make last a long time. She didn't want to waste too much money; a pound already for coming in was enough to spend.

Then people arrived and started to fix up microphones, and the crowd was bigger suddenly and she had to sit squashed up at the end of the seat. Then she saw the Great Gaels having pints of beer at the bar just as if they were ordinary customers. Wasn't Dublin fantastic? You could go into a pub and sit and have a drink in the same place as the Great Gaels. They'd never believe her at home.

The lead singer of the Great Gaels was tapping the microphone and testing it by saying, 'a-one, a-two, a-three . . .' Everyone laughed and made themselves comfortable with full drinks.

'Come on now, attention please, we don't want anyone with

an empty glass now getting up and disturbing us,' the lead singer said.

'No need to worry about that,' someone shouted.

'All right, look around you. If you see anyone who might get thirsty, fill up their glass for them.'

Two men beside Jo looked at her glass disapprovingly. 'What have you in there, Miss?' one said.

'Orange, but it's fine, I won't get up and disturb them,' she said, hating to be the centre of attention.

'Large gin and orange for the lady,' one man said.

'Oh no,' called Jo, 'it's not gin . . .'

'Sorry. Large vodka and orange for the lady,' he corrected.

'Right,' said the waiter, looking at her with disapproval, Jo thought.

When it came, she had her purse out.

'Nonsense, I bought you a drink,' said the man.

'Oh, but you can't do that,' she said.

He paid what seemed like a fortune for it; Jo looked into the glass nervously.

'It was very expensive, wasn't it?' she said.

'Well, we can't always be lucky. You might have been a beer drinker,' he smiled at her. He was very old, over thirty, and his friend was about the same.

Jo wished they hadn't bought the drink. She wasn't used to accepting drinks. Should she offer to buy the next lot of drinks for them all? Would they accept, or, worse still, would they buy her another? Perhaps she should just accept this one and move a bit away from them. But wasn't that awfully rude? Anyway, now with the Great Gaels about to begin, she wouldn't have to talk to them.

'Thank you very much indeed,' she said, putting the orange into the large vodka. 'That's very nice of you, and most generous.'

'Not at all,' said the man with the open-neck shirt.

'It'sh a pleashure,' said the other man.

He was having difficulty saying the letter 's' properly, and Jo realized that both the men were very drunk.

The Great Gaels had started, but Jo couldn't enjoy them. She felt this should have been a great night, only twenty feet away from Ireland's most popular singers, in a nice, warm pub, and a free drink in her hand. What more could a girl want? But to her great embarrassment the man with the open-neck shirt had positioned himself so that his arm was along the back of the seat behind her, and from time to time it would drop round her shoulder. His friend was beating his feet to the music with such energy that a lot of his beer had already spilled on the floor.

Jo hoped desperately that they wouldn't start behaving wildly, and that if they did, nobody would think that they were with her. She had a horror of drunks ever since the time when her family had been invited to Uncle Jim's for a meal. Uncle Jim had picked up the meat from the table and thrown it into the fire because someone had tried to argue with him. The evening had been a complete disaster and as they went home, her father had spoken about drink being a good servant but a cruel master. Her father had said that Uncle Jim was two people, one drunk and one sober, and they were as unlike as you could find. Her father said he was thankful that Uncle Jim's weakness hadn't been noticeable in any of the rest of the family, and her mother had been very upset and said they had all thought Jim was cured.

Sometimes her sisters told her terrible things people had done in the hotel when they were drunk. Drunkenness was something frightening and unknown. And now she had managed to find herself in a corner with a drunk's arm around her.

The Great Gaels played song after song, and they only stopped at the pub's closing time. Jo had now received another large vodka and orange from the friend of the open-shirted man, and when she had tried to refuse, he had said, 'You took one from Gerry – what's wrong with my drink?'

She had been so alarmed by his attitude that she had rushed to drink it.

The Great Gaels were selling copies of their latest record, and signing their names on it as well. She would have loved to have bought it in some ways, to remind herself that she had been right beside them, but then it would have reminded her of Gerry and Christy, and the huge vodkas which were making her legs feel peculiar, and the awful fact that the evening was not over yet.

'I tried to buy you a drink to say thank you for all you bought me, but the barman told me it's after closing time,' she said nervously.

'Is it now?' said Gerry. 'Isn't that a bit of bad news.'

'Imagine, the girl didn't get a chance to buy us a drink,' said Christy.

'That's unfortunate,' said Gerry.

'Most unfortunate,' said Christy.

'Maybe I could meet you another night and buy you one?' She looked anxiously from one to the other. 'Would that be all right?'

'That would be quite all right, it would be excellent,' said Gerry.

'But what would be more excellent,' said Christy, 'would be if you invited us home for a cup of coffee.'

'Maybe the girl lives with her Mam and Dad,' said Gerry.

'No, I live on my own,' said Jo proudly, and then could have bitten off her tongue.

'Well now,' Gerry said brightly. 'That would be a nice way to finish off the evening.'

'I don't have any more drink though. I wouldn't have any beer . . .'

'That's all right, we have a little something to put in the coffee.' Gerry was struggling into his coat.

'Do you live far from here?' Christy was asking.

'Only about ten minutes' walk.' Her voice was hardly above a whisper. Now that she had told them she lived all on her own, she could not think of any way of stopping them.

'It's a longish ten minutes, though,' she said.

'That'll clear our heads, a nice walk,' said Christy.

'Just what we need,' said Gerry.

Would they rape her? she wondered. Would they assume that this was why she was inviting them to her flat – so that she could go to bed with both of them? Probably. And then if she resisted, they would say that she was only playing naughty games with them. And they would force her to give them what they wanted. Was she completely and absolutely mad? She cleared her throat.

'It's only coffee, you know, that's all,' she said, in a strict schoolteacher's voice.

'Sure, that's fine, that's what you said,' Christy said. 'I have a nice little bottle of whiskey in my pocket. I told you.'

They walked down the road. Jo felt terrible. How had she

got herself into this? She knew that she *could* turn to them in the brightly lit street and say, 'I'm sorry, I've changed my mind, I have to be up early tomorrow morning.' She *could* say, 'Oh heavens, I forgot, my mother is coming tonight, I totally forgot, she wouldn't like me bringing people in when she's asleep.' She *could* say that the landlord didn't let her have visitors. But she felt that it needed greater courage to say any of these things than to walk on to whatever was going to happen.

Gerry and Christy were happy. They did little dance steps to some of the songs they sang, and made her join in with the words of the last song the Great Gaels had sung. People looked at them on the street and smiled. Jo had never felt so miserable in her whole life.

At the door she asked them to be quiet. And they were, in a theatrical sort of way, putting their fingers on their lips and saying 'Shush' to each other. She let them in the door and they went upstairs. Please, please God, don't let Nessa and Pauline be in the kitchen. They never are any other night, please don't let them be there tonight.

They were both there. Nessa in a dressing gown, Pauline in a great black raincoat. She was colouring her hair, it seemed, and didn't want bits of the gold to fall on her clothes.

Jo smiled a stiff 'good evening' and tried to hurry the two men past the kitchen door.

'More lovely girls, more lovely girls,' said Gerry delightedly. 'You said you lived by yourself.'

'I do,' said Jo quickly. 'These are the girls from next door. We share a kitchen.'

'I see,' Pauline said in an offended voice. 'We don't have names, we're just the girls from next door.'

Jo wasn't going to explain. If only she could get the two drunks into her own bedsitter.

'What are you doing? Is that your party dress?' Christy asked Pauline.

'No, it's not a party dress, little boy, it's my nightdress – I always go to bed in a black raincoat,' Pauline said and everyone except Jo screamed with laughter.

'I was just going to make us some coffee,' said Jo sharply, taking down three mugs with Visitor painted on them.

Gerry thought the mugs were the funniest thing he had ever seen.

'Why do you put Visitor on them?' he asked Jo.

'I have no idea,' Jo said. 'Ask Nessa.'

'So that you'll remember you're visitors and won't move in to the flat,' Nessa said. They all found this very funny too.

'If you'd like to go into my bedroom – my flat, I mean, I'll follow with the coffees,' Jo said.

'We're having a great time here,' said Christy and pulled out his small bottle from his back pocket.

Nessa and Pauline got their mugs immediately. In no time they were all friends. Christy took out a bit of paper and wrote Christy and Gerry and they stuck the names to their mugs – so that they would feel part of the gang, he said.

Jo felt that the vodka and the heat and the worry had been too much for her. With difficulty, she got to her feet and walked unsteadily to the bathroom. She felt so weak afterwards that she couldn't face the kitchen again. She went to the misery of her bed, and was asleep in seconds.

She felt terrible in the morning. She couldn't understand why people like Uncle Jim had wanted to drink. Drinking made other people look ridiculous and made you feel sick. How could anyone like it? She remembered slowly, like a slow-motion film, the events of the night before and her cheeks reddened with shame. Nessa and Pauline would probably ask her to leave. Imagine coming home with two drunks, and then abandoning them in the kitchen while she had gone away to be sick. God knows who they were, those two men, Gerry and Christy. They might have been burglars even . . . Jo sat up in bed. Or suppose when she had disappeared . . . suppose they had attacked Nessa and Pauline?

She jumped out of bed, not caring about her headache and her stomach pains, and burst out of her door. The kitchen was its usual tidy self: all the mugs washed and hanging back in their places. Trembling, Jo opened the doors of their bedrooms. Pauline's room was the same as ever – huge pictures on the wall and all her punk clothes hanging up in a long line. Nessa's room was as neat as a pin, the bedcover smooth and tidy, a little table with photographs neatly arranged; a little bookshelf with a row of about twenty paperback books. No sign of rape or struggle in either room.

Jo looked at her watch; she was going to be late for work. The other two had obviously gone long ago. But why had they left her no note? No explanation? Or a note asking her for an explanation?

Jo struggled into work, to the anger that met her because she was forty minutes late. Jacinta said to her later on in the morning that she looked really dreadful.

'Really dreadful is exactly how I feel. I think I'm having my first hangover.'

'Lucky you,' said Jacinta jealously. 'I never get a chance to do anything that might give me even a small hangover.'

Jo was terrified of going home. Again and again she practised her apologies. She would blame it on the vodka she had drunk. Or would that be worse? Would they think she was even more awful if they thought she was so drunk last night that she didn't know what she was doing? Should she say that she had been introduced to them by a friend? So she had thought they were respectable people and when she found out that they weren't, it was too late. What should she say? Just that she was sorry.

Neither of them was there. She waited for ages but they didn't come in. She wrote out a note and left it on the kitchen table.

I'm very very sorry about last night. Please wake me when you come in and I will try to give you an explanation. Jo.

But nobody woke her, and when she did wake, it was Saturday morning. Her note was still on the table. They hadn't bothered to wake her. She was such a worthless person that they didn't even want to discuss it.

She made her morning cup of tea and crept back to bed. It was lunchtime before she realized that neither of them was in the flat. They can't have come home last night.

Jo had never felt so uneasy in her life. There must be a perfectly reasonable explanation. After all, the three of them had not made any arrangements to tell each other about their movements. She had realized this on Thursday night. They all lived separate lives. But what could have happened to make them disappear? Jo told herself that she was being ridiculous. Nessa lived in Waterford, or her family did, so she had probably gone home for the weekend. Pauline was from the country too, somewhere. Well, she had to be, otherwise she wouldn't be living in a flat in Dublin. She'd probably gone home too.

It was just chance that they had gone the same weekend. And just chance that they had gone after the visit of the two drunks.

Jo stood up and sat down again. Of course they had to be at home with their families. What else was she imagining?

Go on, spell it out, what are you afraid of, she said to herself. That those two innocent-looking fellows who had a bit too much to drink kidnapped two big strong girls like Pauline and Nessa? Come on! Yes, it was ridiculous, it was bloody silly. What did the men do, point guns at the girls while they tidied up the flat, then put them into a van and drive off with them?

Jo had often been told that she had too much imagination. This was a time when she would have been happy to have no imagination at all. But it wouldn't go away. She couldn't pull a curtain over the worries, the pictures that kept coming up of Christy hitting Nessa and of Gerry with his hands round Pauline's neck. And all the time the same words were going through her mind: 'There must be something wrong, otherwise they would have left a note.'

It was her fourth Saturday in Dublin. The first one she had spent unpacking her suitcase and getting used to the hostel. The second one had been spent looking at flats which were too expensive and too far from work, and which had already been taken by other people. The third Saturday she had spent congratulating herself on having found Nessa and Pauline. And now on this, the fourth Saturday, Nessa and Pauline had most probably been brutally murdered and raped by two drunks that she had brought back to the flat. She imagined herself talking to the guards down at the Garda station.

'Well, you see, it was like this, Officer. I had two large

vodkas in the pub which were bought by these men, and then when we came home – oh yes, Officer, I brought them home with me, why not? Well, when we came home they poured whiskey into our coffees and before I knew where I was I had crashed on to my bed in a drunken sleep and when I woke up my flatmates were gone, and they never came back. They were never seen again.'

Jo cried and cried. They *must* have gone home for the weekend. People did. She had read a big report in the newspaper not long ago about some fellows making a fortune driving people home in a minibus. Lots of country girls, it was said, missed the fun at home at weekends, and this was a good cheap way of getting home.

Nessa and Pauline must have gone off in one of these minibuses. Please, please, St Jude, tell me they've gone home in a minibus. If they went in a minibus, St Jude, I'll never do anything bad for the rest of my life. More than that. More. If they're definitely safe and they went off yesterday in a minibus, St Jude, I'll tell everyone about you. I'll put a notice in the two evening newspapers – and the three daily papers, too, if it wasn't too expensive.

She would bring St Jude's name into everyday conversation with people and say that he was a great man in a crisis. She wouldn't actually describe the whole crisis in detail, of course. Oh dear Lord, speak, speak. Should she go to the guards? Should she make an official report about missing persons, or was she making a huge amount of trouble over nothing? Would Pauline and Nessa be wild with anger if the guards contacted their homes? God, suppose they had *chosen* to go away with the fellows or something? Imagine, if the guards were calling on their families? She'd have put the whole country in a state of alarm for nothing.

But if she didn't get the guards, suppose something had happened because of those drunk men she'd invited into the house. Yes, she, Josephine Margaret Assumpta O'Brien had invited two drunk men into a house, not a week after that nun in the hostel had said that Dublin was a very wicked city, and now her two flatmates, innocent girls who had not invited these men, were missing, with no sign of them whatsoever . . .

She had nothing to eat for the day. She walked around from room to room, stopping when she heard the slightest sound in case it might be a key in the lock. When it was getting dark, she remembered how the men had written their names on bits of paper. They could have taken them away with them, but they might be in the rubbish bin. Yes, there they were, Christy and Gerry, untidily written on bits of paper. Jo took them out with a fork in case they might still have fingerprints on them. She put them on the kitchen table, sat down, and said several long prayers to God.

Outside people passed in the street, getting on with the business of a Saturday night. Was it only last Saturday that she had gone to the cinema with Josie and Helen, those two nice girls in the hostel? Why hadn't she stayed there? It had been awful since she left. It had been frightening and worrying and getting worse every day until . . . until This.

There was nobody she could talk to. Suppose she phoned her sister in the hotel, Dymphna would be really angry with her. Her immediate reaction would be, come-home-at-once, what-are-you-doing-by-yourself-up-in-Dublin, everyone-knew-you-couldn't-manage-by-yourself.

And it was a temptation to run away. What time was the evening train to Limerick? Or tomorrow morning? But she didn't want to go home, and she didn't want to talk to Dymphna and she couldn't explain the whole thing on the phone downstairs in the hall in case the people in the flat below heard – the people in the flat below! *That* was it!

She was half-way down the stairs when she paused. Suppose everything were all right, and suppose St Jude had got them on a minibus, wouldn't Nessa and Pauline be very angry if she had gone in and alarmed the three nurses downstairs? They had said that they didn't talk to them much; the nurses were all right, but it wasn't a good idea to get too involved with them. Yes, well, going in and telling them that you suspected Nessa and Pauline had been kidnapped and mistreated – that was certainly getting involved.

She went back up the stairs. Was there anything that the nurses could do to help that she couldn't do? Answer: No.

Just at that moment the big fair-haired nurse that she had spoken to before came out.

'Hey, I was just going to go up to you girls above,' she said.

'Oh, really, what's wrong?' Jo said.

'Nothing's wrong, nothing at all. We're having a party tonight, though, and we just wanted to say if any of you wanted to come, it starts at . . . well, when the pubs close.'

'That's very nice of you. I don't think ...'

'Well, all we wanted to say is, there may be a bit of noise, but you're very welcome. If you could bring a bottle, it would help.'

'A bottle?' asked Jo.

'Well, you don't have to, but a drop of wine would be a help.'

The nurse was about to walk past her up the stairs.

'Where are you going?' Jo asked, alarmed.

'I've just told you, to ask the others, the ones in the other flats, if they'd like to come . . .'

'They're not there, they're not at home, they've gone away.'

'Oh well, all for the best, I suppose,' the girl said carelessly. 'I've done my social duty now. They can't say they weren't asked.'

'Listen,' Jo said urgently, 'what's your name?'

'Phyllis,' she said.

'Phyllis, listen to me, do the girls up here go away a lot?'

'What?'

'I mean, I'm new here, do they go home for the weekends or anything?'

'I've no idea. I hardly know them at all. I think the punk girl's a bit odd – not quite right in the head. But don't say I said so.'

'But do they go away at weekends or what? Please, it's important.'

'Honestly, I'd never notice. I work night duty a lot of the time. I don't know where I am or whether people are coming or going. Sorry.'

'Would the others know, in your flat?'

'I don't think so, why? Is anything wrong?'

'No, I expect not. It's just, well, I wasn't expecting them to go off and they, well, they have. I was just wondering whether . . . you know, if everything's all right.'

'Why wouldn't it be?'

'It's just that they were with some rather, well, unreliable people on Thursday, and . . .'

'They're lucky they were only with unreliable people on Thursday – I'm with unreliable people all the time! Maureen was supposed to have arranged to borrow the glasses for the party and she didn't, so we had to buy paper cups which cost a fortune.'

Jo started to go back upstairs.

'See you later then. What's your name?' said Phyllis.

'Jo O'Brien.'

'OK, come on down when you hear the sounds.'

'Thank you.'

*   *   *

At twelve o'clock she was wider awake than she had ever been in the middle of the day. Why not go down to the party? It was no worse than staying here. The noise was almost in the room with her. There was no question of sleep.

She put on her black dress and her big earrings, then she took them off. Suppose her flatmates were in danger or dead? What was she doing dressing up and going to a party? It somehow wasn't so bad going to a party without dressing up. She put on her grey skirt and her dark grey sweater, and went downstairs.

She arrived at the same time as four others who had been beating on the hall door. Jo opened it and let them in.

'Which are you?' said one of the men.

'I'm from upstairs, really,' Jo said.

'Right,' said the man, 'let's you and I go back upstairs. See you later,' he laughed to the others.

'No, no, you can't do that, stop it,' Jo shouted.

'It was a joke, silly,' he said.

'She thought you meant it!' The others almost fell over, they were laughing so much.

Then the door of the downstairs flat opened and the heat and noise flooded out into the hall. There were about forty people squashed into the rooms. Jo took one look and was about to run back upstairs again, but it was too late and the door had banged shut behind her. Someone gave her a glass of warm wine. She saw Phyllis in the middle of it all, her fair hair tied up in a knot on the top of her head, and wearing a very fashionable dress with bare shoulders. Jo felt foolish and dull. She was packed into a group of bright-faced, laughing people, and she felt as grey as her sweater and skirt.

'Are you a nurse too?' a boy asked her.

'No, I work in the post office.'

'Well, can you do anything about the telephones? Do you know there isn't a telephone between here and . . .'

'I'm not interested in stupid telephones,' Jo said and pushed away from him. Nessa and Pauline were dead, murdered by drunks, and here she was talking about telephones to some fool.

'I was only making conversation – you silly cow,' he shouted at her, offended.

Nobody heard him in the noise.

'Which are your flatmates?' Jo asked Phyllis.

'The one in the kitchen, Maureen, and the one dancing with the man in the white sweater, that's Mary.'

'Thanks,' said Jo. She went into the kitchen.

'Maureen,' she said. The girl at the cooker looked up with a despairing face. 'I wanted to ask you . . .'

'Burned to death, both of them. Both of them burned to bloody death.'

'What?' said Jo.

'Two pans of sausages. Just put them in the oven, it's easy,

Mary says. I put them in the oven. And now look, burned black. Jesus, do you know how much they cost, and there were two and a half kilos altogether. I told her we should have fried them. The smell will be terrible if we fry them, she said. Well, what will this do, I ask?'

'Do you know the girls upstairs?' Jo said.

'No, but Phyllis said she asked them. They're not making trouble, are they? That's all we need.'

'No, I'm one of them. That's not the problem.'

'Thank God. What will I do with these?'

'Throw them out, pans and all, I'd say. You'll never get them clean.'

'Yes, you're right. God, what a disaster. What a mess.'

'Listen, do you know the girls, the other ones, Nessa and Pauline?'

'I know what they look like. Why?'

'Do you know where they are?'

'What? Of course I don't. If they're here, they're in the other room, I suppose, waiting to be fed, thinking there's some hot food. I'll *kill* Mary, I'll really *kill* her, you know.'

'Do they normally go away for the weekend?'

'God, love, I don't know whether they go up to the moon and back for the weekend. How would I know? There's one of them with a head like a searchlight and another who goes round with labels putting names on anything that stands still . . . bells and doors and things. I think they're all right. We never have many dealings with them. That's the best way in a house of flats, I always say.'

Jo didn't go on. It seemed unlikely that Mary would know any more, and she decided to leave her happily dancing with the man in the white sweater until she was given the bad news about the sausages.

A hand caught her and suddenly she was dancing herself. The man was tall and had a nice smile.

'Where are you from, Limerick?'

'Very nearly right,' she said laughing. Then terror took hold of her again. What was she doing dancing with this stranger and chatting him up like she might have done at a dance at home?

'I'm sorry,' she said to him, 'I'm sorry, I have to go. I've got something awful on my mind. I can't stay.'

At that moment the window in the kitchen was broken by a big stone, and broken glass flew everywhere. There were screams from the garden and shouts.

'I'm getting the guards. This looks like a bad fight,' said the tall boy and like a flash he was out in the hall. Jo heard him speaking on the phone. In the kitchen people were shouting to each other to move carefully. A huge lump of glass lay balanced on top of a cupboard; it could fall at any moment.

'Is anybody hurt, stop screaming, is anybody cut?' Jo recognized Phyllis and felt a small amount of relief flood back into her. At least they were nurses; maybe a lot of them were. They would know what to do better than ordinary people. People had run out of the front door and a fierce argument was going on in the garden. Two men with cut heads were shouting that they only threw the stone in self-defence. People had started firing things at them from the window first; one of them was bleeding over his eye. They only picked up the stone to stop things being thrown at them.

The guards were there very quickly, four of them. Suddenly everything was different; what had looked like a party began to

At that moment the window in the kitchen was broken by a big stone, and broken glass flew everywhere.

look like something shameful. It had been a room full of smoke and drink and music and people dancing and people talking about nothing. Now it was a room full of broken glass and overturned chairs and people shouting, trying to explain what had happened, and people trying to comfort others, or get their coats and leave. Neighbours had come in to protest and stare: it was all different.

It didn't take long to work it out: the two men in the garden had not been invited. They had tried to come in the front door and had been refused admittance. They had then gone around to see if there was a back entrance. That was when the first one had been attacked with a hot weapon which had both burned and cut his face. The other man, coming to investigate the attack, had been wounded in exactly the same way. (The weapons were, of course, Mary's burnt sausages.) The two men thought that everybody in the party was firing things at them so they threw one stone before leaving.

Notebooks were being put away. Phyllis said that one of the men needed attention for his cut, and she would go to the hospital with him, taking Mary as well, since Mary's arm had been cut by flying glass. The party was over. The guards said that too much noise was being made for a residential area and, since two of the hostesses were disappearing to the hospital, there didn't seem to be any point in guests staying on in a flat which was now full of icy winds because of the window. Some of the men helped to pick the last bit of broken glass out, and a sheet of thin metal was found to put over the hole. It was a sad end. The guards were leaving; one of them saw Jo sitting on the stairs.

'Are you all right for a lift home?' he asked.

Jo shook her head. 'I don't need one. I live upstairs.'

'You look a bit shaken. Are you all right?'

She nodded wordlessly.

'What a night. Not much of a Saturday night in Dublin for a little country girl, is it?'

He was trying to cheer her up. It didn't work.

'Well, I'll be off. You go off too and get some sleep. You need it by the look of you.'

She nodded again.

'You are all right, you're not in shock or anything? It's all over. It was only a broken window,' he said gently. 'There'll be worse things than that before the night's over.'

'Oh God,' she said.

'Hey, Sean,' he called, 'this one's going to faint, I think. Give me a hand.'

Jo opened her eyes as they were getting her in through the door of the flat. She had had the key in her hand and it had fallen when she fell.

'Which is her room?' Sean said.

'How would I know?' said the one who was carrying her. 'Here's the kitchen, get her in there . . .'

Jo saw the names on the table.

'Don't touch those, they're evidence,' she said. 'Please don't touch them.'

They decided they'd better all have a cup of tea.

*　　*　　*

'It's television, that's what it is,' Mickey said.

'It's that and eating too much rich food late at night,' said Sean.

'But how can you be sure they're all right?' Jo wasn't convinced.

40

'Because we're normal human beings,' said Sean.

Jo's face went red. 'So am I. I'm normal too, that's why I'm worried. I'm just concerned and worried about them. Stop making horrible jokes about my eating rich food and having bad dreams. I haven't eaten anything, I'm so worried. And that is exactly why I didn't come to the Garda station because I knew that's the kind of reception I'd get.'

She burst into tears and put her head down on the table.

'Mind the evidence,' said Sean laughing.

Mickey frowned at him. 'Leave her alone. She *is* worried. Listen here, those two will be back tomorrow night as right as rain. Nobody kidnaps people like that, honestly. Nobody says please wash up all the mugs and tidy up your rooms and come on up the Dublin mountains to be kidnapped, now do they?' He smiled at her encouragingly.

'I suppose they wouldn't.'

'And you're kind to be concerned, and we'll say no more about it tonight because you're exhausted. Go to sleep and stay in bed tomorrow morning. Those two girls will be home tomorrow night and you'll think you were mad crying your heart out over them. Do you hear me?'

'But I'm so stupid, I'm so hopeless. I can't manage on my own in Dublin, I really can't. I thought I'd have a great time when I got a flat, but it's all so different, and so lonely, so terribly lonely, and when it isn't lonely it's like a bad dream . . .'

'Now stop that,' Mickey said firmly. 'Stop it at once. You never talk about anyone except yourself, I this, I that. You're constantly wondering what people are thinking about you. They're not thinking about you at all.'

'But I . . .'

'There you go again. I, I, I. You think that there's a crowd of people watching you, sitting there as if they were in the cinema, watching you leave the house each day, watching all your movements, saying, is she having a good time, is she being a success in Dublin? Nobody even gives it a thought. Why don't you start thinking about other people?'

'But I *am* thinking about other people. I'm thinking about Nessa and Pauline . . .'

'Oh no, you're not. You're only thinking about what *you* did to them, whether *you're* responsible for their kidnapping and disappearance, or whether they'll think *you're* silly.'

Jo looked at him.

'So, lesson over. Go to sleep.' He stood up. So did Sean.

'You're probably right,' she said.

'He's always right. Well known for it,' said Sean.

'Thank you very much indeed, it is a bit lonely at first. You get self-centred.'

'I know. I felt a bit the same last year.'

'You come from Sligo?'

'Galway.'

'Thank you very much again.'

'Goodbye, Jo.'

'Goodbye, Guard, thank you.'

'Mickey,' he said.

'Mickey,' she said.

'And Sean,' Sean said.

'And Sean,' Jo said.

'And maybe some night you might come out with me,' said Mickey.

'Or me, indeed?' said Sean.

'I saw her first, didn't I?' said Mickey.

'You did,' said Jo. 'Indeed you did.'

'I'll wait a bit until the two girls are back, but I've a night off on Monday . . .'

'You're sure they'll come back?'

'Maybe if I called for you about eight on Monday? How's that?'

'That's grand,' said Jo. 'That's really grand.'

MURMURS IN MONTROSE

Seven people woke up that morning and remembered that this was the day Gerry Moore came out of the nursing home. He wouldn't be cured, of course. You were never cured if you were an alcoholic. Four of the people shook their heads and thought that perhaps he wasn't really an alcoholic – it was just descriptions that had changed. There was a time when a man had a drop too much to drink, but now it was all medical, and in the blood and the way the body worked, and there were illnesses and diseases that had never existed before. Two people knew very well that he was an alcoholic. And the seventh one, waking up that morning, looking forward to his release, had never believed for one moment that there was anything wrong with Gerry. He had gone into that nursing home for a good rest, and that's all there was to it.

*   *   *

Gerry's mother was seventy-three, and there had never been any shameful gossip about her family before, and there wasn't going to be any. She had brought up five boys on her own. Three of them were abroad now, all of them earning a good salary. Only two were in Ireland, and of those Gerry was easily her favourite.

A big innocent man without a bit of harm in him. He worked too hard, that was the problem and in his job, Gerry had told her often, the best place to meet customers was in pubs. A grown man couldn't sit like a baby in a pub, drinking a pint of orange juice! Naturally a man had to drink with the people he talked to. They wouldn't trust him otherwise. His health had broken down from all the long working hours, that's what he had told her. He had to go into the nursing home for six weeks for a total rest. No one was to come and see him. He would be out in the first week of May, he had said. Now it was the beginning of May and he'd be home, as right as rain. That's if anyone could be as right as rain in the house his precious Emma looked after for him. Stop. She mustn't say a word against Emma; everyone thought Emma was the greatest thing since sliced bread. Keep quiet about Emma. Even her son Jack had said that Emma was a walking saint. Jack! Who never noticed anyone . . .

* * *

Jack Moore woke up that morning with a heavy feeling in his chest. He couldn't identify it for a while. He went through the things that might cause it. No, he had no argument going on with Mr Power in the office; no, he had no great bag of dirty clothes to take to be washed. No, there had been no bill from the garage for his car – and then he remembered. Gerry came home today. He had insisted on taking a bus home in his own time; no, he didn't want anyone to collect him, didn't want to look like a wheelchair case. Anyway, he had to start taking control of his own life again. Jack knew that the visit to the nursing home was going to be a big talking point for Gerry, a bit of excitement, an amusing story to be told. It would be just like when Gerry lost his driving licence. They had all listened fascinated while Gerry told his story of the young guard asking him to blow into the bag. The jokes that Gerry had made had brought smiles even to the faces of the guards. It hadn't done any good in the end, of course. The bag that Gerry had blown into had shown he had more than five times the legal limit of alcohol in his blood. He had been put off the roads for a year. Emma had taken twenty-five driving lessons in ten days; she had passed her driving test. She drove the car, remembering to take the keys out of it when she was going to leave both the car and Gerry at home. Emma was a saint, a pure saint. Jack hoped her children appreciated her.

*   *   *

Paul and Helen Moore woke up and remembered that this was the day that Daddy came home. They were a lot more silent at breakfast than usual. Their mother had to remind them of the good news. When they got back from school, their Dad would be sitting at home as cured from his disease as he could hope to be. Their faces were serious. But they should be cheerful, their mother told them; everything was going to be fine now. Dad had gone of his own choice into a place where they gave him tests and rest and treatment. Now he knew that drinking alcohol for him was like drinking poison, and he wouldn't do it.

Paul Moore was fourteen. He had been going to go and play in his friend Andy's house after school, but that wouldn't be a good idea now. Not if a cured father was coming back. Paul never asked his friends to come and play in his house. Well. It was only one day.

Helen Moore was twelve. She wished that her mother didn't go *on* about things so much, with that kind of false, bright smile. It was really better to be like Father Vincent, who said that God arranged things the way God knew best. Father Vincent believed that God thought it was best for Dad to be drunk most of the time. Or that's what it seemed that Father Vincent thought. He never seemed too certain about anything.

*   *   *

Father Vincent woke wishing that Gerry Moore had a face that was easier to read. He had been to see him six times during his cure. By the end Gerry had been the most cheerful patient in the nursing home. The nurses, nuns, and other patients had all been fascinated by his stories of the people he had photographed, the adventures, the mistakes corrected just in time, the disasters avoided at the last minute. Alone with the priest, Gerry had put on a serious face the way other people put on a raincoat; temporarily, not considering it as anything to be worn in real life. Yes, Gerry had understood the nature of his illness, and wasn't it bad luck – a hell of a lot of other fellows could drink as much as he drank and it never bothered them. But he would have to give it up. Oh well. But then the priest had heard him tell stories about photographing film stars, and meeting famous people face to face. He never seemed to remember that he hadn't done a book for four years, and that for two years nobody had commissioned any photographic work from him at all. He had spent most of his time drinking with that friend of his from the television station, the fellow who seemed able to get his work finished by twelve noon and spend the rest of the day in Madigans bar. A hard man, poor Gerry used to call him.

48

Des the hard man. Father Vincent hoped that Des-the-hard-man would be some help when Gerry came out of the nursing home. But he doubted it. Des didn't look like the kind of man who would be a support to anybody.

✻   ✻   ✻

Des Kelly woke up at five a.m. as he always did. He slipped out of the bed so as not to wake Clare; he had become quite expert at it over the years. He kept his clothes in a cupboard on the stairs so that he could dress in the bathroom without disturbing her. In half an hour he was washed, dressed and had eaten his breakfast cereal; he took his coffee into the study and lit the first cigarette of the day. God, it was great that Gerry was being released from that place at last; the poor devil would be glad to be out. Des had been up once to visit him and he'd known half the crowd in the sitting room, or half-known them. Gerry wasn't well that day, so Des had written a quick note to say he'd called. He'd felt so helpless, since his automatic response had been to leave a bottle of whiskey. Still, it was all over now, and no harm done. They'd cleaned all the poison out of him, told him to keep off the alcohol for a bit longer, then go easy on it. Or that's what Des supposed they told him; that made sense, anyway. If the drink did as much damage as it had done to poor old Gerry over the last few months, it was wiser to stop it for a bit. What annoyed Des was all this ridiculous nonsense about Gerry having an illness. There was no healthier man in Dublin than Gerry Moore. He had been a bit unfortunate. But now he had time to sort himself out and make plans for his work; well, he'd be back on top in no time. That's if know-all Emma, expert-in-everything Emma, didn't take control of him and squash the remaining life out of him. Gerry would need to be careful. With a friend like that boring priest Father Vincent, with a miserable-faced brother like Jack and with know-all Emma for a wife, poor Gerry needed a couple of real friends. Des and Clare rarely agreed about anything these days, but they both agreed it was a real mystery that a grand fellow like Gerry Moore had married that Emma. Des sighed at the puzzle of it all and got out his papers; he always got his best work done at this time of the morning.

*   *   *

Emma woke up late. She had hardly slept during the night but had fallen into one of those heavy sleeps just before morning. She was sorry now that she hadn't got up at six o'clock when she was so restless; the extra three hours weren't worth it. She jumped out of bed and went to the sink in the corner. She didn't wash much; just gave herself what her mother called a lick and a promise. She smiled at the way she had accepted the expression for so long and never questioned it until today. Today of all days she was up late and examining her face in the mirror, wondering what old childhood sayings meant. She pulled on her pale blue sweater and jeans and ran downstairs. Paul and Helen looked at her as accusingly as if she had sent them away to a children's home.

'We had to get our own breakfast,' said Helen.

'You'll be late for work,' said Paul.

'The place looks awful for Daddy coming home,' said Helen.

Biting her lip hard to stop herself shouting at them, Emma managed a sort of smile. The children had spilt water, hot and cold, all over the kitchen. Good God, it's not that difficult to fill an electric kettle and then to pour hot water into cups of instant coffee, is it? She didn't say it, she didn't ask the obvious question which would result in excuses and argument and more excuses. They had spread coffee powder everywhere, put butter on the sink as well as their bread, there were little bits of bread all over the table . . . Keep calm, keep calm.

'Right, if you've had your breakfast, you get off to school, and we'll have a celebration supper tonight. Isn't it wonderful?' She looked brightly from one to the other.

'Why didn't you get up in time, Mummy, if it's such a wonderful day?' Helen asked. Emma felt that she would like to smack her daughter hard.

'I was awake most of the night and I fell into one of those heavy sleeps just a short time ago. Come on now, love, you should be gone . . .'

'Will the celebration supper last long? Can I go over to Andy's house afterwards?' asked Paul.

'Yes!' said Emma sharply. 'When supper's over, you can do what you like.'

'Is Father Vincent coming to supper?' Helen asked.

'Heavens, no. I mean, who would have asked him? Why do you think he might be here?' Emma sounded alarmed.

'Because he's often here when there's a crisis, isn't he?'

'But this isn't a crisis. This is the end of the crisis. Daddy is cured, I tell you, cured. All the awful things about his disease are gone. There's no need for Father Vincent to come and be helpful.'

'You don't like Father Vincent much, do you?' said Helen.

'Of course I do, I like him very much. I don't know where you got that idea. It's just that he's not needed tonight.' Emma was wiping and cleaning and putting things into the sink as she spoke.

'Would you say that you like Father Vincent less or more than you like Dad's friend Mr Kelly?' asked Helen.

Emma stopped cleaning and folded her arms. 'Right, is there anything else you'd like to do before you go to school? Play hide-and-seek? Maybe we could have a few games of cards as well or do some word puzzles? Will you get yourselves . . .'

They laughed and ran off. She ate the bits of bread they had left, washed the cups and plates and ran from the kitchen into the sitting room. The children had been right; it was a mess. She took a deep breath and made a big decision. One hour would make all the difference. Please God, let someone nice answer the phone, someone understanding, who realized that she wasn't just being lazy or unpunctual.

'Hallo, is that RTE? Can you put me through to . . .' No, suddenly she put the phone down. It was bad enough having one person in the family who let people down. She had never missed a day's work since she had got the secretarial job in Montrose, and she wasn't going to miss even an hour today. She tidied up the worst of the mess, pushing newspapers and magazines into the cupboard, gathering any remaining cups or glasses from last night. Gerry wasn't the kind of person who noticed what a place looked like.

She threw out the worst of the flowers and changed the water in the vase. Then she took out her Welcome Home card and wrote 'from all of us with love'. She put it up against the flower vase, ran out pulling the door shut behind her, jumped on her bicycle and set off for Montrose. Because she was a little later than usual there was more traffic, but she didn't mind; she thought of it as a battle. She would fight the cars and the traffic lights and the bits of road that were uphill. She would think about nice things, like how she had lost ten kilos in weight in two months; how she could get into jeans again; how someone had really and truly thought she was a young woman, not the forty-year-old mother of teenagers. She thought of how she would lie in the sun and get beautifully brown next summer; she thought that she might have her hair colour lightened a little if it wasn't too expensive. She thought of everything in the world except her husband Gerry Moore.

*   *   *

Gerry Moore was so popular in the nursing home that they were all sorry to lose him. The nurses all told him that and so did the patients. The doctor had his last little talk with him that morning and said that in many ways Gerry had been one of the most successful patients who had ever done the programme because he had refused to let it depress him.

'You've been so cheerful and good-tempered all the time, Gerry, that you've actually helped other people. I must admit that at the start I was less than convinced. I thought you were just passing the time until you could get out and get at the drink again.'

'I would have to be half mad to do that, wouldn't I?' Gerry said. The doctor said nothing.

'I know, I know, a lot of the fellows you get in here are half mad. But not me. Honestly, I know what I'm doing now. I just have to change my habits, my way of life, that's all. It can be done. I once had a way of life, a grand way of life, without drink. I'll have one again.'

53

'You'll be in here giving us lessons soon,' the doctor laughed.

Gerry had several people to say goodbye to; he promised he'd come back to see them.

'They all say that,' people said, but people believed that Gerry Moore would; he was that kind of man.

Nurse Dillon said she was surprised that a man like Mr Moore, with so many friends of his own, didn't want anyone to come and collect him. Gerry had put his arm around her shoulder as she walked with him to the door.

'Listen to me. I'm thinner, I'm much more handsome, I'm a sensible man now, not a madman. I'm a great fellow now compared to the way I was when I walked in. So don't you think I should go home my own route and let the world have a look at me?'

She waved to him all the way to the end of the road. He was a lovely man, Mr Moore, and actually he was right. He did look fantastic now. You'd never think he was an old man of forty-five.

'Take care of yourself as you go your own route,' she called.

*　　*　　*

His own route. Now where would that have taken him in the old days? Stop remembering, stop pretending it was all wonderful . . . a taste was only a taste, it wasn't anything special. He knew that. Stop trying to make it exciting. These pubs, the ones he might have called into, they weren't welcoming corners where friends called him to join their circles. Some of them were dirty and depressing. If occasionally he had got into conversation with anyone, it would have been with an unfriendly depressed man who might have looked at him with suspicion. It was only when he got back nearer home that he would find people he knew in pubs. Friends. Stop pretending it was wonderful. It had *not* been all the time people calling out to him: 'There's Gerry, just the man we want, come on over here, Gerry, what'll you have?' No, it hadn't been like that. People had avoided him, for God's sake, in the last months. He knew that, he had had to face up to it. People he had known for years. Boy, wasn't it going to be a shock for them when they saw him with his big glass of orange juice or tonic water or lemonade? Ho, they'd be surprised . . . never thought old Gerry Moore had a strong enough character to give up drinking.

Gerry walked to the bus stop. He had a small suitcase. He hadn't needed much in hospital, just his night clothes and a wash bag, really; a couple of books and that was it. Why had his suitcases always been so heavy in the old days? Oh, of course, bottles of booze in case he was ever in a place where there was nothing to drink, and his photographic equipment. No more attention to booze *EVER* again, but a lot of attention to work. He was looking forward to spending a good month sorting himself out and seeing where he was, then another month writing to lots of possible customers, offering specialized work. By midsummer he should have as much work as he used to have, and more.

A bus came and he got into it. Happily, he reached into his pocket and got out the money Emma had brought him. He hadn't wanted money but of course he had been brought into the nursing home penniless. Emma had given him money for tipping and taxis or whatever he needed. He hated taking her money, he hated that more than anything.

He got off the bus in the city centre. Other people were

walking about normally, it seemed to him; they had no problems and big decisions. They looked into shop windows, or narrowed their eyes against the sunlight, trying to see whether the traffic lights were red or green. A few early tourists wandered slowly around; everyone else seemed to be more in a hurry. Gerry looked at them curiously. Most of them would have no problems with drinking a few glasses of whiskey, a few beers, a bottle of wine with their meal. But a lot of them wouldn't even bother to drink anything.

He saw with annoyance a couple of men pass by who wore little pins on their jackets; members of the Give-up-drink-for-God crowd. The idea of giving up alcohol as a sacrifice to God always annoyed Gerry deeply. Most of these fellows didn't know what they were giving up. It was as if he said that he would give up grapefruit or horsemeat, something he'd hardly ever tasted. God couldn't be all that pleased with such a sacrifice. God, if he was there at all, must know that these fellows were just insincere and boastful.

Steady, now, steady. Stop thinking about drink as some wonderful creator of happiness. Don't imagine that a drink suddenly turns the world into a better, brighter place. The world's fine now, isn't it? He didn't want a drink at this moment, did he? No. Well then, what was the problem?

He caught the number ten bus just as it was about to drive away. There right in front of him was Clare Kelly.

'The lovely Clare . . . well, aren't I lucky?' he said, putting on his most charming smile for the whole bus to see.

Clare was embarrassed and annoyed by this unexpected meeting. Gerry could see that. She was a distant, cold sort of woman, he had always thought. Always had a sharp, clever answer on her tongue. Gave poor Des a bloody awful time at home. Des had nothing to say to her these days, he had often told that to Gerry. He had said that he and Clare didn't actually talk, or have real conversations. There was always a state of war, where one or the other was winning. Nobody could remember when the war had started but it was there, in private as well as in public, trying to score points against each other all the time. Not that there was much in public these days. Clare didn't have much time for her husband's friends. Des preferred it that way. Let her have her meetings and her own life; let her laugh and make clever, unkind remarks with her own friends. That suited him fine. Gerry had been very sorry for Des, the best of fellows. It didn't matter what things went wrong in his own life, at least Emma didn't laugh unkindly at him.

Clare had moved over to make space for him. 'You're looking great,' she said.

'Well, I should, shouldn't I, as it cost so much,' he said, laughing. 'Can I get your ticket? Two to . . . are you going home or are you off to do good works in the world somewhere?' He paused as the bus conductor waited.

'Home,' she laughed at him. 'You haven't changed, Gerry. They didn't knock the life out of you in there.'

'No, only the booze,' he laughed happily, and gave her the bus ticket as though he was giving it to a child. 'Here, take this in case we have a fight before we get home and you and I separate.'

'Are you on your way home now from . . . you know?'

'Yes, just released. They gave me back my own clothes, a few pounds to keep me going, and the names and addresses of people who might employ an ex-prisoner . . .' He laughed, but stopped when he noticed that Clare wasn't laughing at all.

'Wouldn't you think that Emma . . .? It's awful to have you coming out on your own, like this.'

'I wanted to. Emma said she'd come in the car after work, your Des said he'd come for me in a taxi, Brother Jack, cheerful as ever, said he'd arrive and accompany me home after work, Father Vincent said he would come with a saint's uniform and fly me home on a cloud . . . but I wanted to come home on my own. You could understand that, couldn't you?'

'Oh yes,' said Clare, managing in just two words to sound bored rather than sympathetic.

'Well, how's everything been, out in the real world?'

'Quiet, a bit quieter without you.' She didn't smile as she said it. She said it as though he were a dangerous influence, someone who had been upsetting people. She hardly bothered to hide her regret that he was back out in the world. He smiled at her pleasantly as if he hadn't understood the meaning behind her words. He had to be very calm, no point in becoming over-sensitive, or seeing insults, or taking offence, or thinking people were being unfriendly. There must be no running away to hide because people were embarrassed about his treatment; no rushing out to comfort himself because the world didn't understand. Nice and easy.

'Ah, if that's the case, we'll have to bring a bit of excitement into it. A quiet world is no use to God, man, or the devil, as they say.' He said no more on this and drew her attention to some building work they could see from the bus. 'Hey, that reminds me,' he said cheerfully, 'did you hear the story about the Irish bricklayer who came in to this building site looking for a job . . .'

Clare Kelly looked at him as he told the story. He looked thinner and his eyes were clear. He was quite a handsome man in a way. Of course it had been years since she had seen him sober so that made a difference. She wondered, as she had wondered many times, what people saw in him; he had no brain whatsoever. In between his ears he had solid wood.

She smiled politely at the end of the story, but it didn't matter to Gerry because the bus conductor and three people nearby had laughed loudly. And he was really telling the joke to them as much as to Clare.

*   *   *

He was pleased to see the flowers. That was very nice of Emma. He put his little suitcase down in the sitting room and moved automatically to the cupboard under the music centre to pour himself a drink. He had his hand on the door when he remembered. God, how strong the old habits were. How ridiculous that in all those weeks in the hospital he never found himself automatically reaching for some alcohol, but now here at home . . . He remembered that nice young Nurse Dillon saying to him that he would find it hard to make the normal movements at home because he would be so used to connecting them with drink. She had said that some people invented totally new things to do, like drinking Bovril when they came into the house. Bovril? He had wrinkled his nose. Or any unfamiliar drink, like lemon tea or hot chocolate. She had been very nice, that Nurse Dillon. She saw the whole thing as a bit of bad luck, like catching a bad cold. She had even given him a small bottle of Bovril last night and said that he might laugh now but he could find that he needed it. He had said that he was such a

59

strong character he would go to the drinks cupboard and pour the bottles down the sink. Nurse Dillon said that he might find his wife had already done that for him.

Gerry opened the cupboard doors. Inside there were six large bottles of lemonade, six of tonic water, six of Coca Cola. There was a bottle of orange drink and several tins of tomato juice. He stared at them for a moment. So Emma had taken responsibility for him, and had poured away all his alcohol without even bothering to ask him. He felt his neck turning red with anger. In fact, she had taken too much bloody responsibility. What was it she had said about trusting him, and relying on him, and letting him make his own decisions? What did all that mean if she had poured his drink away? There had been several bottles of wine, and two bottles of whiskey there. Money to buy things didn't grow on trees.

Very, very upset he went out to the kitchen and put his hands on the sink deliberately to relax himself. He looked down into the sink. Without a word of discussion she had poured about twenty pounds worth of drink down there. Then his eye fell on a box in the corner of the kitchen, with a piece of writing paper stuck to it.

Gerry. I took these out of the sitting-room cupboard to make room for the other lot. Tell me where you want them put. E.

His eyes filled with tears. He wiped his face with the back of his hand and swallowed as he lit the gas to boil the kettle to make his cup of Bovril.

*   *   *

Mrs Moore had rung once or twice during the day, but there had been no reply. That Emma and her precious job. What was

Emma had poured away all his alcohol.

she except an ordinary typist, really? Just because she worked with all those famous radio and television people in Montrose; just because she had sat at the same table as Gay Byrne in the coffee shop, and had walked down a corridor with Mike Murphy; just because she had given Valerie McGovern a lift in her car and had a long conversation with Jim O'Neill from Radio Two . . . Oh yes, they were all famous names, but did that make her special? Oh no, it didn't, just a clerk is all she was. And a clerk with a heart of stone. The girl had no feeling in her. Wouldn't any normal person have taken the day off work to welcome her husband back from six weeks in hospital? But not Emma. The poor boy had to come back to an empty house.

'Ah, there you are, Gerry. How are you, are you feeling all right now, did you have a good rest?'

'I'm feeling great, mother, really great. Ready for anything.'

'And did they give you medicines, did they look after you properly? I can't think why you didn't go to Vincent's hospital. You live so close to it. And you could have gone there free, with the government health service.'

'Oh, I know, mother, but they don't have the course there. I had the whole course, you know, and thank God it seems to have worked. But of course, you never know. You're never really sure.'

'What do you mean you're not sure? You're all right! They had you in there for six weeks, didn't they? Gerry? Do you hear me? If you don't feel all right, you should see someone else. Someone we know.'

'No, mother, I'm fine, really fine.'

'So what did they tell you to do, rest more?'

'No, quite the opposite, in fact. Keep busy, keep active, get really tired out.'

'But that was the reason you had to go in there, wasn't it, because you were tired out and needed a rest?'

'You know as well as I do why I had to go in there. It was the drink.'

His mother was silent.

'But it's all right now. I know what I was doing to myself and it's all over.'

'A lot of nonsense, they talk. Don't let them get you involved with their courses, Gerry. You're fine, there's nothing the matter with you, you can have a drink as well as the next man.'

'You're not helping me, mother. I know you mean well but those are not the facts.'

'Facts, facts . . . don't bother with *your* facts, with *their* facts up in that place. The fact is that your father drank as much as he liked every evening of his life and he lived to be seventy, God have mercy on him. He would have lived to be far more if he hadn't had that heart attack.'

'I know, mother, I know, and you're very good to be so concerned, but, believe me, I know best. I've been listening to them for six weeks. I can't touch drink any more. It's labelled poison as far as I'm concerned. It's sad, but there it is.'

'Oh, we'll see, we'll see. A lot of modern rubbish. Emma was explaining it to me. A lot of nonsense. People had better things to do with their time when I was young than to be reading and writing these reports about not eating butter and not smoking and not drinking. Wasn't life fine in the old days before all these new worries came to trouble us, tell me, wasn't it?'

'It was, mother, it was,' said Gerry tiredly.

* * *

It *had* been fine for a while. When Gerry and Emma got married he had a good career. There was a lot of money to be made from advertising in the sixties: one day he had been photographing a bottle and an attractive glass, another day he had been giving advice about photographing new banks, the offices, the employees, the buildings. He had known all the photographic agencies; there was no shortage of work. Emma had been so enthusiastic about his work – she had said it was much more exciting and alive than her own. She had taught financial bookkeeping and accountancy for beginners in a technical school. She never called it a career. She had been delighted to leave it when Paul was expected, and she had never seemed to want to go back when Helen was off to school and out of the way, and that was at least seven years ago. Now that the bottom had fallen out of the market in advertising and there were no good photographic jobs left, Emma wasn't able to get back into teaching either. They didn't want people who hadn't worked for fifteen years; why should they? That's why she was up in the television station doing typing, and thinking herself lucky to get the job.

They had said in the nursing home that it wasn't very helpful to look back too much on the past; it made you feel sorry for yourself, or sad. Or else you began to realize that what had happened was predetermined, you couldn't have prevented any of it. And that wasn't a good idea either. You started to think you had no responsibility for your actions. So let's not think of the past, the old days when life was fine. He made the Bovril and took it, smelling it suspiciously, into the sitting room. Hard not to think of the old days. There was the photo of their wedding;

laughing and healthy, both of them. His own father and both Emma's parents, now dead, smiled out from more formal photos. His mother had looked confident, as if she knew she would live a long time.

Then the pictures of Paul and Helen, the ones that he had taken. The photos looked wonderful, people said, hanging on the back wall of the sitting room; they were a record of children in the 1970s growing up, turning into people before your eyes. But the photographic record had stopped about five years ago, and it seemed as if the children had stopped growing up too. They seemed trapped in the past, unable to exist in the present.

He looked back at the wedding picture and again he felt his eyes beginning to fill with tears, as when he read Emma's note in the kitchen. Poor girl, she was only a girl. She was only thirty-nine years old and she had been keeping four people for two years on a typist's salary. That was the truth of the matter. Of course, there had been the occasional cheque coming in for him: a bit of money from the sales of some of those big photographic books he had done; a little here for a print of an old photo he'd taken, a little there for permission for reprints. But he had cashed those cheques and spent the money himself. Emma had paid for all the family expenses. God, he would repay her for everything, he really would. He would repay every penny and every hour of worry and anxiety. He wiped his eyes again, he must be big and strong. Gerry Moore was home again, he was going to take over his family once more.

*   *   *

Emma hadn't liked to make a phone call while the office was quiet. It was too important a call; she couldn't suddenly hang up if she felt that people were listening to her. Anxiously she watched the clock, knowing that he must be home by now, wishing that she had done more to make the place welcoming, checking off in her mind the shopping she had done at lunchtime. She was going to make them a celebration meal. She hoped he wasn't regretting his decision to come home alone. Going back to an empty house, to a changed way of life after six weeks in a hospital, it wasn't such a good idea. To her great delight the office filled up with people and she was able to turn her back and call home.

'Hello?' His voice sounded a little hesitant, and even as if he had a cold.

'You're very welcome home, love,' she said.

'You're great, Emma,' he said.

'No, I'm not, but I'll be home in an hour and a half and I can't wait to see you. It's grand you're back.'

'The place is great. Thank you for the flowers and the card.'

'Wait till you see what we're going to eat tonight – you'll think you're in a first-class hotel.'

'I'm cured, you know that.'

'Of course I do. You're very strong and you've got a wonderful life ahead of you, we all have.'

His voice really did sound as if he had a cold, but maybe he was crying – she wouldn't mention it in case it was crying and it upset him that she noticed.

'The children will be in any minute; you'll have them to talk to soon.'

'I'm fine, I'm fine. You're very good to ring. I thought you couldn't make phone calls there.' She had told him that the television company had absolutely forbidden private calls in or out. She had said this to stop him ringing when he was drunk.

'Oh, I took a risk with one today, because today is special,' she said.

'I'll soon have you out of that place, never fear,' he said.

She remembered suddenly how much he hated her being the breadwinner for the family.

'That's great,' she said. 'See you very soon.'

She hung up. He sounded grand. Please, please, God, let it be all right. There was a man in RTE who hadn't touched a drop of alcohol in twenty years, he told her. A lovely man, great fun, very successful, but he said he was always in dreadful trouble when he was a young fellow. Maybe Gerry would be like him. She must believe. She must have trust in him. Otherwise the cure wouldn't work.

* * *

Paul came home first. He felt a bit awkward when he saw his father sitting reading the *Evening News* in the big armchair. It wasn't just six weeks since he had seen such a sight, it was much longer; Dad hadn't been around much for a long time.

He put down his books on the table.

'You're back, isn't that great?' he said.

Gerry stood up and went and put both hands on his son's shoulders. 'Paul, will you forgive me?' he asked, looking straight into the boy's eyes.

Paul felt his face turning red. He had never been so embarrassed. What was Dad saying these awful emotional things for? It was worse than some awful old film on the television. Would he forgive him? It was enough to make you feel quite sick.

'Sure, Dad,' he said, slipping away from the hands. 'Did you get the bus home?'

'No, seriously, I have been very anxious to say this to you for a few weeks, and I'm glad to have a chance before there's anyone else here.'

'Dad, it doesn't matter. You're fine now, and that's the only important thing, isn't it?'

'No, of course it isn't. There's no point in having a son unless you can talk to him. I just want to say that for too long this house hasn't been my responsibility. I was like someone who ran away, but I'm back, and it will all be like it was when you were a baby and don't remember . . . but this time you're grown up.'

'Yes,' said Paul, confused.

'And if I start telling you when to do your homework or to help in the house, I don't expect you to obey my orders without a murmur. You can say to me, why the hell should you give us orders? Where were you when we needed you? I'll listen to you, Paul, and I'll answer. Together we'll make this a proper family.'

'I wouldn't say things like that. I'm glad you're home, Dad, and that it's cured, the illness thing, honestly.'

'Good boy.' His father took out a handkerchief and blew his nose. 'You're a very good boy. Thank you.'

Paul's heart sank. Poor old Dad was in a terrible state; maybe his mind had gone to pieces in that place, talking all this emotional rubbish, and tears in his eyes. Oh bloody hell, now he couldn't ask to go over to Andy's house. It would cause a huge upset and maybe his father would burst into tears. God, wasn't it depressing.

*   *   *

Helen went into the priest's house on her way home in order to speak to Father Vincent.

'Is anything wrong?' The priest immediately assumed the worst.

'No, Mummy keeps saying there's no crisis, so it must be all fine, but I came to ask you if you'd call in tonight on some excuse. If you could make up some reason why you had to call . . .'

'No, child, your father's coming home tonight. I don't want to interrupt the first family meeting; you'll all want to be together. Not tonight. I'll call in again sometime, maybe in a day or two.'

'I think it would be better if you came in now, at the beginning, honestly.'

The priest was anxious to do the best thing but he didn't know what it was. 'Tell me, Helen, what would I say, what would I do? Why would I be a help? If you could explain that to me, then I would come, of course.'

Helen was thoughtful for a moment. 'It's hard to say, Father Vincent, but I'm thinking of other times. Things were never so bad when you were there. They used to put on some manners in front of you, you know, Mummy and Daddy; they wouldn't be fighting and saying awful things to each other.'

'Yes, but I don't think . . .'

'Perhaps it didn't look very great to you, but if you weren't there, Daddy would be drinking much more and saying awful things and Mummy would be shouting at him not to upset us . . .'

The child looked very upset; Father Vincent spoke quickly. 'I know, I know, but that sort of thing happens in a lot of homes. Don't think yours is the only one where people shout at each other, you know. But you're forgetting one thing, Helen, your father is cured. Thank God he took this cure himself. It was very hard and the hardest bit was having to admit that he couldn't control his drinking. He now has admitted this and he's fine, he's really fine. I've been to see him, you know, up in the nursing home. I know he didn't want you children going there, but he's a new man; in fact, he's the old man, his old self, and there won't be a thing to worry about.'

'But he's still Daddy.'

'Yes, but he's Daddy without drink. He's in excellent shape, you'll be delighted with him. No, I won't come in tonight, Helen, but I'll give a ring over the weekend and maybe call round for a few minutes.'

Helen looked rebellious. 'I thought priests were meant to help the community. That's what you always say when you come up to the school to talk to us.'

'I am helping, by not interfering. Believe me, I'm older than you are.'

'That's the thing people say when they've no other argument,' Helen said.

＊　　＊　　＊

Emma cycled down the road and saw Helen moodily kicking a stone.

'Are you only coming home now?' she asked, annoyed that Helen hadn't been back to welcome Gerry earlier.

'I called in to see Father Vincent on the way,' said Helen.

'What about?' Emma was alarmed.

'Private business, you're not supposed to ask people what goes on between them and their priest. What's said in confession is secret.'

'Sorry,' said Emma. 'He's not coming round here tonight by any awful chance, is he?'

Helen looked at her mother with a puzzled look. 'No, he's not, actually.'

'Good, I want us to be on our own today. You run ahead and say hello to your father. I'll be in in a minute.'

Unwillingly Helen walked on. As she turned in at the gate, she saw her mother take out a comb and mirror and pat her hair. How silly Mummy could be at times. What was she combing her hair for now? There was nobody at home to see her. Why hadn't she combed it when she was in RTE where she might meet people who'd be looking at her?

*   *   *

Gerry hugged Helen so hard that she could hardly breathe.

'You're very grown up, you know, a real teenager,' he said.

'Oh Dad, it isn't that long since you've seen me, it's only a few weeks. You sound like an old sailor coming back from months abroad.'

'That's what I feel like, that's exactly the way I feel – how clever of you to notice it,' he said.

Helen and Paul exchanged fairly alarmed glances. Then they heard Mum's bicycle banging against the garage wall and everyone looked at the back door. She burst in through the door and into the kitchen. Her face was pink from riding the bicycle; she had a huge bag of shopping which she had taken from the

They hugged each other in the kitchen.

basket on the bicycle. In her jeans and shirt she looked very young, Gerry thought.

They hugged each other in the kitchen, swaying backwards and forwards as if the children were not there, as if Gerry wasn't holding a second mug of Bovril in his hand, and as if Emma wasn't holding the shopping in hers.

'Thank God, thank God,' Gerry kept saying.

'You're back, you're back again,' Emma said over and over again.

Wide-eyed, their children looked at them from the door into the hall. Their faces seemed to say that this was almost as bad as what they had had to put up with before.

*   *   *

The telephone rang as they were having supper. Emma, her mouth full of fish, said she'd answer it.

'It's probably your mother. She said she'd ring.'

'She has,' said Gerry.

It was Jack. He had been kept late at the shop. Mr Power had decided at the last moment that all the furniture in the showrooms should be moved around so that the cleaners could clean the places they couldn't usually get at. Emma spent two and a half minutes listening to a fierce attack on Mr Power; she made agreeing noises and comforting murmurs. Then Jack's voice changed and became confidential.

'Is he home?' he whispered.

'Yes, thank God, he came home this afternoon. Looks really well. We'll all have to go up there and be spoilt and looked after, I tell you.' She laughed and sounded light-hearted, hoping Jack would catch her mood.

'And is there . . . is there any sign of . . .?'

'Oh yes, very cheerful, and he sends you his good wishes – we're just having a welcome home supper for him actually.' Would Jack understand what she was saying, was there the slightest chance that he might realize he had rung at a meal-time?

'Is he listening to you, there in the room?'

'Yes, that's right.'

'Well, I obviously can't talk now. I'll ring later, when he's asleep maybe.'

'Why don't you ring in the morning, Jack, say, late morning. Saturday's a good day. We'll all be around then, and you could have a word with Gerry himself. Right?'

'I'm not sure if I'll be able to ring in the late morning.'

'Well, sometime tomorrow . . .' She looked back at Gerry. They smiled at each other and raised their eyes to the ceiling. 'If only you'd get a phone, we could ring you. I hate you always having to find the coins for calls.'

'There's no point in paying the rental for a telephone, and they charge you any figure that comes into their heads, I tell you, for the number of calls. No, it's better to use the pay phone, it's not far away. The only trouble is there's often a lot of kids around on a Saturday.'

'Well, whenever you can, Jack.'

'You're wonderful with him, wonderful. Not many women would be able to manage like you.'

'That's right,' she laughed. He was such a lonely person that she didn't like to cut him off too quickly. 'And how are you keeping yourself?' she asked.

Jack told her. He told her that he had a bad neck which

resulted from a cold wind that came through a door which Mr Power insisted on being open. He told her that people weren't buying as much furniture as they used to, and that this enthusiasm for buying second-hand furniture from old houses was a disaster for the business. Emma made a sign to Paul, who was nearest to her, to pass her plate. She was annoyed with Jack's timing and his insensitivity, but if she hung up she would feel guilty. And tonight of all nights she wanted to be able to relax without another problem crowding her mind.

She looked over at the table as she let Jack talk on and on. They all seemed to be getting on all right. Gerry looked great, he had lost weight too. The two of them were much more like their wedding photograph than they had ever been. His face was thinner, his eyes were bright, he was being endlessly patient with the kids, too, which was a lot more difficult than it sounded. Helen in particular was nervous and moody, and Paul was restless. Jack seemed to be coming to an end. He would ring tomorrow and talk to Gerry. He hoped Gerry appreciated all she did for him, going out and earning a living, keeping the family together. Why hadn't he had more common sense long ago, and not put so much at risk?

'But it's all fine now,' Emma said patiently. Jack agreed doubtfully and hung up.

'Was he apologizing for my wicked life?' asked Gerry.

'A bit,' Emma laughed. Gerry laughed, and after a moment the children laughed too. It was the nearest to normal living they had known for about four years.

*　　*　　*

Gerry spent Saturday in his study. It was a four-bedroomed

house and when they had bought it they had decided at once that the big bedroom should be his study. Other men rented offices, so it was only sensible that the big bedroom with the good light should be where Gerry worked. The little bathroom attached to the bedroom was turned into a photographic darkroom. Once it had all been really well organized: a huge old-fashioned chest of drawers, a lovely piece of furniture, which held all his neatly arranged records. The chest was as efficient as any modern metal office furniture, and a hundred times more attractive. The lighting was good, the walls were hung with pictures: some of a single object, like his famous picture of a diamond; some were pictures that told a success story. Gerry winning a prize here, Gerry sharing a joke there. Then there was the huge, untidy desk, full recently of bills or information sheets, or refusals or rubbish. It was difficult to remember how neat and efficient it had all been.

He had sighed when he saw it, but Emma had been beside him.

'Tell me what you want except a couple of black plastic sacks to get rid of the rubbish,' she had said.

'And a bottle of booze to get rid of the pain of looking at it,' he had said.

'You poor old devil, it's not that bad, is it?' she said lightly.

'No,' he said, 'I'm only joking really. But I'll need several plastic bags.'

'Don't throw everything out,' she said, alarmed.

'I'll throw a lot out, love. I have to start again from the beginning, you know that.'

'You did it once, you'll do it again,' she said and went downstairs.

*   *   *

Gerry decided to make four big heaps: Real Rubbish; Rubbish
for Looking Through Later; Things to be Put Away, and
Contacts for the New Life.

Almost everything seemed to fit into one or other of those.
He was pleased with himself and even sang a little as he set to
work sorting everything out.

Emma heard him as she made the beds and she paused and
remembered. Remembered what it used to be like: a cheerful,
confident Gerry, whistling and singing in his study, then
running lightly down the stairs and into his car off to another
job. In those days there was a big notebook beside the phone
where she put down the time when the person called, their
name, their business. She had always sounded so efficient and
helpful; customers had often asked if she was Mr Moore's
partner and she would laugh and say a very permanent partner
– they had found that entertaining. For months, years, the
phone had hardly rung for Gerry, except a call from Des Kelly
or a complaint from his brother Jack, or a list of complaints
about something from his mother. Should she dare to believe
that things were ever going to be normal again? Was it really
possible to believe that he would stay off the drink and build up
his business? She didn't know. She had nobody to ask, really.
She couldn't go to Alcoholics Anonymous and discuss it with
other wives and families, because that somehow wasn't fair. It
would be different if Gerry had joined Alcoholics Anonymous;
then she would be able to join some support group attached to
it, but no. Gerry didn't want to go to some room every week and
hear a lot of bores standing up and saying, 'I'm Michael, I'm an

alcoholic.' No, the course was the modern way of dealing with things and he had done that and been cured.

She sighed. Why was she blaming him? He had done it his way and he had done it. For six weeks in that nursing home he had become stronger and more determined. For two days at home now he was managing. She must stop feeling uneasy and suspicious and afraid, afraid of things like the first phone call from Des Kelly, the first quarrel, the first disappointment. Would he have the strength to go on being cheerful after all these?

＊　　＊　　＊

Gerry had taken down three bags of Real Rubbish into the garage, all neatly tied at the neck. He insisted that Emma come up and admire what he had done. The room still looked to be in a mess to her, but he seemed to see some system in it, so she was enthusiastic about it. He had found three cheques as well – out of date, but they could be re-dated. They totalled over £200. He was very pleased with himself for finding them and said that they could afford to go out for dinner somewhere.

'Are you sure that they haven't already been replaced by later cheques? One's three years old.' Emma wished she hadn't said it. It sounded rather unkind. She went on quickly. 'If they have been, so what? You're quite right. Where shall we go?'

He suggested a restaurant which was also a pub. She kept the smile on her face unchanged. There was going to be a lot of this kind of thing. She'd better learn to get used to it. Just because Gerry Moore had to cut alcohol out of his life, it was ridiculous to hope that the rest of Ireland would decide to stop selling it, serving it and advertising it.

'I'd love that,' she said enthusiastically. 'I'll wash my hair and find something different to wear.'

Des Kelly rang a bit later.

'How are you, old friend?' he asked.

'Ready for the Olympics,' Gerry said proudly.

'Do they include a few glasses of orange juice somewhere, or would going to a pub be a bit hard for you?'

'Oh, I don't have any problems with going to a pub, but not tonight – I'm taking Emma out for a special dinner to say thank you.'

'Thank you?'

'For taking charge and looking after everything while I was away in that place.'

'Oh yes, of course, of course . . .'

'But tomorrow, Des, as usual. Twelve thirty?'

'That's great. Are you sure you won't . . .'

'I'm sure, I'm sure. Tell me about yourself – what have you been doing?'

Des told him about a piece of writing which he had worked really hard on which had been refused by some stupid fool in RTE who knew nothing. And he told him about another piece that had gone well and been praised in the newspaper reports.

'Oh yeah, I remember that. That was before I went in,' Gerry said.

'Was it? Maybe it was. The time gets confused. Well, what else? The same as usual. I've missed you, old son, I really have. Things have been quite dull, really. I tried leaving Madigan's and I went to McCloskey's and I went down to the Baggot Street area for a bit, Waterloo House, Searson's, Mooney's, but there was no one to talk to. I'm glad you're out.'

79

'So am I.'

'Did they give you a hard time in there?'

'Not at all, they were fine. I was free to decide for myself. If I didn't want to do something, I didn't have to.'

'Well, that's good.'

'And you can relax. I'm not going to turn serious and start giving you advice and telling you that you should cut down the drinking a bit.' Gerry laughed as he said it. Des laughed too, with some relief.

'Thank God for that. See you tomorrow, old son, and enjoy the special night out.'

Gerry wished that he had found cheques for two thousand pounds, not two hundred. Then he would have taken Emma on a holiday. Maybe when the work was going well again, he'd be able to do that. He'd think about it. It would be great to rent a villa for two weeks in one of those places like Lanzarote in the Canary Islands. There was a fellow in the nursing home who had bought a house there with a whole group of other Irish people. They made their own fun, they brought out a car full of tax-free booze – well, forget that part of it, but there were wonderful beaches and lovely weather even in winter.

He went back to sorting out his study. It was the contacts that were giving him the most trouble. A lot of agencies seemed to have changed, been taken over by others or gone out of business. A lot of new names. A lot of bad dealings with some of the old names – work promised and not done, work done but not accepted. Jesus, it might be easier starting again in another country. Australia? Dublin was like a village; what one person knew at lunchtime everyone else knew at tea time. Still, nobody had said it was going to be easy.

*   *   *

Gerry was in a very depressed mood when the time came to get dressed for going out. The children were out of the house: Paul was with Andy as usual, and Helen had gone to a tennis lesson. She had asked that morning at breakfast if the family finances would cover tennis lessons. She didn't really mind if they didn't, and she wasn't going to make a nuisance of herself. But if the money was there, she would like to join the tennis group. Gerry had insisted that she joined, and said that he would get her a new tennis racket if she learnt to play well. Helen had departed in a very cheerful mood and would stay and have tea with one of her friends who lived nearby.

Emma was fixing her newly washed hair. She sat at the dressing table in the bedroom and watched Gerry come in. At first she had thought he might want them to go to bed. They hadn't made love last night; they had just lain side by side holding hands until he gradually fell asleep. This seemed like a good time. But no, that was the last thing on his mind so she was glad he hadn't noticed her inviting smile. It didn't seem so hurtful if he hadn't understood what she was suggesting. His face looked moody and cross.

'It will be nice to go out. I'm really looking forward to it,' she said brightly.

'Don't start reminding me of my failures. I *know* you haven't been out for a long time,' he said.

She bit her lip hard to stop an angry reply. 'What will you have, do you think?' she said, searching desperately for something pleasant to say that would not start an argument.

'How the hell do I know until I see the menu? I don't have

81

magic eyesight that can read things two miles away. I don't receive messages from God to tell me what's going to be served.'

She laughed. She felt like throwing her hairbrush and every single thing on the dressing table at him. She felt like telling him what to do with his dinner invitation – a dinner she would have to pay for anyway until those out-of-date cheques were cashed . . . if they ever were. She felt like saying that the house had been a peaceful and better place while he was in the nursing home. But she managed to say, 'I know. It's because I'm such a greedy person, I expect. Don't mind me.'

He was shaving at the small sink in their bedroom. His eyes caught hers and he smiled. 'You're too good for me.'

'No I'm not, I'm what you deserve,' she said lightly.

In the car he took her hand.

'Sorry,' he said.

'Don't worry about it,' she said.

'The evening ahead of us just seemed rather hard, not much to look forward to – no wine with the dinner.'

'I know,' she said sympathetically.

'But you're to have wine, you must; otherwise the whole thing is a nonsense.'

'You know I don't mind one way or the other. You know I can easily have tonic water.'

'Part of being cured is not to mind if other people are drinking. It was just that I got a bit depressed there, inside, in the house, I don't know. I'm fine now.'

'Of course you are, and I'll certainly have a glass or two if it doesn't annoy you.' She started the engine and drove off.

Officially, he was allowed to drive again now, but he hadn't applied for his new licence, or whatever you were supposed to do. And in the last few months he wouldn't have been able to drive. She had offered him the keys as they came to the car and he had shaken his head.

In the bar, as they looked at their menus, they met a couple they hadn't seen for a while. Emma saw the wife whisper to her husband and point over at them. After a long careful stare he came over to them.

'Gerry Moore, I haven't seen you looking so respectable for years. And Emma . . .'

They greeted him with little jokes and little laughs; both of them patted their flatter stomachs while the man said they must have been at a health farm because they looked so well. Emma said that she had lost weight because of all her cycling and Gerry said that, sadly, he had lost his because he had given up the booze. It was like winning the first small battle in a long struggle. Emma knew from the whispers between the couple that there would be many more. The news would get around; people would come to inspect, to see if it was true. Gerry Moore, that poor old boozer, back to his former self, you never saw anything like it, doesn't touch a drop now, made a fortune last year, back on top as a photographer, you never saw anything like him and his wife. Please. Please, God. Please let it happen.

*   *   *

Father Vincent called around on Saturday night and knocked for a long time at the door. The car was gone, Emma's bicycle was there, and there was no reply. He assumed that they must all be out on some family visit. But that child had seemed so white and worried, he hoped that Gerry hadn't gone back to drinking immediately and been taken back into the nursing home. He had a long discussion with himself about whether to leave a note or not. In the end he decided against it. Suppose poor Gerry had gone back to drinking and been taken back in, it would be a terrible thing to leave a welcome home card. Father Vincent wished, as he often did, that he had the power to see into the future.

Paul came home from Andy's and turned on the television. Helen came in soon afterwards; they sat with sandwiches and glasses of milk and watched happily. They heard voices, and a key turn in the lock.

'Oh God,' said Paul, 'I'd forgotten *he* was back. Pick up the glass, Helen, give me those plates. We're meant to be keeping the home neat and tidy!'

Helen laughed at the imitation of her father's voice, but she looked out into the hall anxiously to make sure that Daddy wasn't drunk.

＊　　＊　　＊

It was very expensive having Gerry home. Emma realized this, but couldn't quite think why. She realized that he wasn't spending any money on drink. Apart from that one Saturday night out they didn't spend money on restaurant meals or inviting friends to dinner. Gerry bought no clothes or things for the house. Why then was her money not stretching as far as it used to? A lot of it might be on paper and envelopes and stamps. Gerry was keeping his promise about writing to people with ideas – just bright, cheerful letters which said, without going into detail, I'm back, I'm cured, and I'm still a great photographer.

He liked to cook new things, things that he wouldn't connect with alcohol. Together they had spent a great deal of money on all the things needed to make Indian dishes, but then he had got tired of it all, and said it wasn't worth all the trouble. They could go out and buy a good Indian meal if they needed one. She wasn't angry at the waste, but she had been so used to counting every penny carefully, putting this little bit there towards the electricity, this towards the gas, and that towards the phone. She didn't know what she was going to do when the next bills came in. And talking of bills, what the phone bill was going to be like made her feel weak around the legs.

Gerry had been talking to somebody in Limerick for nearly fifteen minutes one night, and he mentioned calls to Manchester and London. She had said nothing; she just prayed that all these phone calls had brought in enough results and rewards by the time the telephone bill came in.

*   *   *

Gerry's mother thought that he wasn't his usual self at all since he came out of that place. He had gone up to see her and the visit was not a success. She had bought a little bottle of whiskey for him specially. It was in the glass-fronted cupboard there beside the ornaments. Ah, go on, surely one drink wouldn't do him any harm.

'No, Mother. That's the whole point. I've got something wrong with my insides. Alcohol turns to poison in me. I told you this. Emma explained . . .'

'Huh, Emma. Clever talk. A lot of nonsense and long medical words. I'm fed up with it.'

'Yes, Mother, so am I,' Gerry's patience was slipping away, 'but it happens to be true.'

'Look, have just the one and we'll stop fighting,' his mother had said.

'It would be easy for me to say "Thank you, Mother", to hold it here in my hand and when you weren't looking to throw it away. But I can't do that. I can't bloody do it. Can't you put some sense into your silly head and try and understand that?'

'There's no need to shout at me. I've quite enough to put up with,' his mother had said, and then she had started to cry.

'Listen, Mother, give me the bottle you so kindly bought for me. I'll give it to Father Vincent for one of his church activities. He can use it as a competition prize or something. Then it won't be wasted.'

'I will not. If I bought whiskey, it will be there to offer to someone who has the good manners to take it.'

No more was said about the whiskey but whatever they talked about, there was the same lack of understanding and sympathy between them. Gerry left, and hoped that nobody who lived on earth had such a terrible relationship with a parent as he had. That was the day that he went home and found Paul fighting with Emma in the kitchen. They hadn't heard him come in.

'But WHY, if you could tell me WHY, then I might do it,' Paul was saying. 'He's not sick, he's not soft in the head, so why does he want to play happy families sitting down to supper together every night? If I go over to Andy's house after supper it's too late, then the evening's spoiled.'

'Ask Andy here.'

'You must be joking. I'd never do that.'

Gerry came in and looked at them, first one and then the other.

'Please spend the evening with your friend tonight, Paul. Emma, can I have a word with you in my study when you're ready?'

He walked on upstairs. He heard Helen, giving a nervous little laugh.

'That's just the voice that our Headmistress uses when she's going to throw someone out of school,' she said, trying to hide her laughs.

*　　*　　*

In the study Gerry turned to face Emma when she came in. 'The boy is right. I am not soft in the head. I get tired of all these family meals, if you must know.'

'But I'm out all day and you're getting back into a routine and I thought . . .'

'You thought, you thought, you thought . . . what else is it in this house except what you think?'

She looked at him in disbelief.

'I mean it, Emma, morning, noon and night . . .'

Two large tears fell down her face and two more were on the way down like raindrops on a window. She didn't even brush them away; she didn't try to deny it, to reason with him, or to agree with him. She just looked beaten.

'Well, say something, Emma. If you don't agree with me, say something.'

'What is there to say?' she sobbed. 'I love you so much and everything I do seems to hurt you. Dear God, how can I do what will please you? I'm obviously doing all the wrong things.'

He put his arms around her and stroked her hair. 'Stop, stop,' he said. She cried into his chest.

'You're very good. I'm just a bastard, a real bastard.' She made a tearful denial into his shirt.

'And I love you too and need you . . .'

She looked up at him with a tear-stained face. 'Do you?'

'Of course,' he said.

Downstairs, Helen said, 'They've gone into the bedroom. Isn't that peculiar?'

Paul said, 'He can't be going to throw her out of school then.'

Helen said, 'What do you think they're doing?'

Paul laughed knowingly. 'I'll give you one guess,' he said.

Helen was horrified. 'They can't be. They're much too old.'

Paul said, 'Why else have they closed the door?'

'God, that's awful. That's all we need.'

Father Vincent called just then. Helen was so embarrassed when she recognized his shape through the door that she ran back for Paul.

'I can't tell him what we think,' she said. 'You couldn't tell a priest something like that.'

Paul let him in. 'Mum and Dad are upstairs at the moment, having a bit of a rest. If you don't mind, Father, I won't disturb them.'

'Of course, of course.' Father Vincent looked confused.

'But can I get you a cup of tea, coffee?' Paul went on.

The priest said he didn't want to be any trouble.

'A drink?' offered Paul.

'No, no, heavens, no.'

'We have drink. Dad insists that it's kept in the house for visitors.'

Father Vincent stayed for about ten minutes with no drink and hardly any conversation. When he was at the front door again, he looked nervously at the stairs. 'If your father has begun to have some problems and your mother wants any help, she only has to ask me.'

Paul said that he didn't think Mother wanted any help just now. When the door was safely closed, he and Helen rolled around the sitting room floor, laughing at the idea of leading Father Vincent upstairs, knocking on the bedroom door and calling out that Father Vincent wanted to know if Mother wanted any help or if she could manage on her own.

Gerry and Emma lay in their big bed and Gerry said, 'It's been so long, I was afraid to, I was afraid, in case . . .'

Emma said, 'You were lovely as you were always lovely.'

She lay counting the days; she was safe, she had to be safe. The idea of becoming pregnant, now, was too awful to think about. She had stopped taking the pill two years ago. It was said to have some bad effects and women were warned not to keep taking it for ever. And what on earth had been the point of taking the pill when there was simply no risk of becoming pregnant?

*   *   *

Jack was sorry that Gerry was back. It had put a stop to his Monday visits. He used to visit Gerry on a Sunday and then took the bus to their house on a Monday night after work to report on what he saw, what he said, what was said back to him and what he thought. The first couple of times they had been eager to know what he reported because they still hadn't got used to life without Gerry. Then, after that, it had become a pleasant routine. Emma used to cook a nice meal, and then they would all wash up. Jack would sit down in the comfort of a nice big sitting room, not his own narrow little bedsitter. They used to watch television, while Emma sometimes mended clothes; the television was turned down low so as not to disturb the two children who were doing homework. All through April and May Jack had been involved in their life. There was no excuse for him to come any more.

He had liked those evenings sitting there with Emma. She had been so nice and interested in everything he had been doing at work. It was so comfortable, so comforting. Gerry must have been a madman, completely crazy to throw away all his money and his good career and spend time drinking with a crowd of fools. You wouldn't think so badly of a man who had nothing at home . . . but a man who had Emma. It was just impossible to understand.

*   *   *

It seemed a very long summer for everyone. Father Vincent spent a lot of time wondering what he had done to offend the Moores. Every time he went there those two young children, who had seemed nice and normal previously, were always laughing in an extremely silly way. Gerry had told him sharply that he wanted to hear no encouraging stories of how other people had succeeded in giving up drink. And Emma was too busy to say more than hello, how are you. She had started to do typing work at home, as well as her job at RTE, and had phoned him once to ask if there was any paid work for the local church. He had said that they would always be glad of some unpaid help, but she had said sorry, she was not yet in a position to be able to offer that.

Mrs Moore thought that Gerry had become quick-tempered

and impatient. Her grandchildren never came near her, and that Emma seemed to be too busy even to talk to her on the telephone.

Paul fell in love with Andy's sister, but Andy's whole family, sister and all, went to Greece for a month. If Paul had two hundred pounds, he could have gone out to visit them. His dad had said he could bloody earn it if he wanted it, and his mum had said he must be a selfish little pig to think money like that was available for a holiday for him.

Helen was very bored and very worried. She had become very ugly suddenly, she thought, after years of looking quite nice. Now, when it was important, she had become disgusting-looking. In books people's mothers helped their daughters when this kind of thing happened. They lent them make-up and bought them dresses. In real life her mum told her to stop complaining and feeling sorry for herself. When she was older she could start worrying about make-up and clothes.

Des felt the summer was long too. He had nothing but admiration for Gerry. Gerry sat there in the pub just as he used to, bought his share of drinks like any other fellow; but it wasn't the same. Des couldn't relax like he used to; he couldn't get it out of his mind that he was waiting for Gerry to start, to catch up with the rest of them. It was restless drinking with him. God knows, Gerry was very extreme. When he really let himself go, he was a fierce drinker; he'd got them thrown out from several bars. But now he'd had a fright, and instead of taking it nice and easy like any normal person and just being careful, here he was like a bloody saint, sitting there with a glass of lemon and tonic or whatever he drank nowadays.

Gerry found the summer slow. He found the replies to his

letters even slower, and the offers of any work were the slowest of all. How could the whole photography world have gone to pieces without his noticing it? There must be people getting work; he saw their pictures in the advertisements, on the television, in the magazines.

'Maybe,' Emma had said, 'maybe you should show them what you can do *now*, rather than collections of old photos. Maybe you should get a new collection together for another book?'

But did Emma have any idea at all how long it took to put a book together? You didn't go out with a camera and just take 150 photos and then mark them pages one to one hundred and fifty. There had to be some connecting idea, some purpose behind it all. There had to be a commission: a lot of the pictures in his other books had been done and paid for already in somebody else's time. Oh, it was all so slow getting back, and it had seemed so very fast, the fall down the ladder. But had it really been so fast? Or was he just pretending to himself that it had been?

Emma realized one day during that endless summer that she had no friend. Not a single one. There was nobody she could talk to about Gerry. There never had been. Her mother had thought Gerry was unsuitable for her, and her father had wondered if he was financially reliable. But whoever she had married, her parents would have worried about exactly the same things. She never talked to her sister about anything except her sister's five children, all of whom seemed to be doing extraordinarily well in exams at any time of the year. She couldn't talk to Gerry's mother; she certainly couldn't talk to that Des Kelly, who always looked at her as if she were a particularly dangerous kind of snake. Poor Jack was so kind and anxious to help, but really the man was not very intelligent; he couldn't have a serious conversation about Gerry's future however hard he tried. She had begun, quite unreasonably, to dislike Father Vincent, who used to be a good friend of theirs ten years ago. He had always been quick to be sympathetic and understanding towards weakness, but that was not what she needed now.

She needed particular advice. It was now four months since Gerry had come out of that nursing home; he had not earned one penny from his profession of photography. To complain about that seemed impatient and ungenerous because, after all, the man had not touched one drop of alcohol either. There was no point in going to the nursing home and asking the doctors. They had asked her to be helpful and undemanding. She thought that she was doing that part of it. But dear God, how long would it go on? Already the number of small debts was growing; strangely, this was more frightening than when he had been drinking and the bill from the shop would arrive. Those drink bills had been terrifyingly unreal. Today's bills, for the telephone, for photography equipment, for printing costs, for expensive pieces of meat – all these had a very permanent feel to them. And Emma wanted to know how long to go on. How long did he have to be encouraged, supported, given time to get back his confidence in himself? How soon, in other words, could she tell him that there was a job in a photographer's in town? It was a very ordinary, low-class photography job for the great Gerry Moore, but she knew that the man who owned the shop needed an assistant. Did she dare yet to tell Gerry, suggest it to him, say that it would be a good idea for a year or two and he could build up his contacts after work? No, it must be too soon, otherwise why would she feel sick at the stomach even thinking about it?

That September they went to a wedding. They didn't know the people well and in fact they were rather surprised at the invitation. When they got there and discovered that they were among four hundred people, it became clear that it was a big social event. A lot of money was being spent to make sure that the guests had a good time.

'Isn't it wonderful to give two kids a wedding like this – they'll remember it all their lives,' Gerry had said. Something about the way he spoke made Emma look up sharply from her plate. She stared at his glass. He was drinking champagne. She felt the blood go out of her face.

'It's only a little champagne for a wedding,' he said. 'Please. Please, Emma, don't start criticizing me, don't start telling me it's the beginning of the end.'

'Gerry,' she gasped at him.

'Look, it's a wedding. I don't know people, I'm not relaxed, I'm not able to talk to them. Just three or four glasses and that's it. It's all *right*, tomorrow it's back to the everyday business of lemonade and tonic water.'

'I beg you . . .' she said. He had held out his glass to a passing waiter.

'What do you beg me?' His voice had turned hard and there was an ugly little smile on his face as well. 'What could you possibly beg from me – you who have everything?'

His voice was loud now and people were beginning to look at them. Emma felt her stomach begin to tie itself into knots from terror – the kind of terror she had known as a child when riding a bicycle too fast downhill. That was what it felt like now. Fast and terrifying and not knowing what lay ahead.

'Could we go home, do you think?' she asked faintly.

'It's only beginning,' he said.

'Please, Gerry, I'll give you anything.'

'Will you give me champagne, and fun and a bit of a laugh? No, you'll give me criticism and a flood of tears and then if I'm very good, a piece of meat pie.'

'No.'

'What, no meat pie? Oh, that decides it, I'll have to stay here.'

She whispered, 'But the whole life, the plans . . . the plans. Gerry, you've been so good. Dear God, five months and not a drop. If you were going to have a drink, why here, why at this place, why not with friends?'

'I haven't any friends,' he said.

'Neither have I,' she said seriously. 'I was thinking that not long ago.'

'So.' He kissed her on the cheek. 'I'll go and find us some.'

He was sick three times during the night, coughing noisily into the sink in their bedroom. Next morning Emma brought him a pot of tea and a packet of headache pills, half a grapefruit and the *Irish Times*. He took them all weakly. There was a picture of the young couple at the wedding they had been to. They looked smiling and happy. Emma sat down on the bed and began to pour tea.

'Hey, it's after nine. Aren't you going to work?' he asked.

'Not today. I'm taking the day off.'

'Won't you get into trouble?'

'I don't think so. Not for one day.'

'That's the problem employing married women, isn't it?

They have to stay at home and look after their babies.'

'Gerry.'

'You told them you'd no babies, but still here you are staying at home looking after one.'

'Stop it, have your tea . . .'

His shoulders were shaking. His head was in his hands. 'Oh God, I'm sorry, poor poor Emma, I'm sorry. I'm so ashamed.'

'Stop now, drink your tea.'

'What did I do?'

'We won't talk about it now while you feel so awful.'

'I must know.'

'No worse than before, you know.'

'What?'

'Oh, it's hard to describe. General noisiness, a bit of singing. A bit of telling them that you had had the cure and you were in control now – drink was your servant, not your master . . .'

'Jesus.'

They were silent, both of them.

'Go to work, Emma, please.'

'No, it's all right, I tell you.'

'Why are you staying at home?'

'To look after you,' she said simply.

'To do guard duty,' he said sadly.

'No, of course not. It's your decision, you know that well. You're not my prisoner. I don't want you to be.'

He took her hand. 'I'm very very sorry.'

'It doesn't matter.'

'It does. I just want you to get inside my head. Everything was so dull and grey and hopeless. Same old thing. Dear Johnny, I don't know whether you remember my work. Dear Freddie.

Dear Everybody . . .'

'Shush, stop.'

'No thanks, I'll have a tonic water, no, thanks, I don't drink, no, seriously, I'd prefer a non-alcoholic drink, nothing anywhere, nothing, nothing. Do you blame me for trying to cheer life up a bit, just once, with somebody else's champagne? Do you? Do you?'

'No, I don't. I didn't realize it was so grey for you. Is it all the time?'

'All the bloody time, all day, every day.'

She went downstairs then and sat in the kitchen. She sat at the kitchen table and decided that she would leave him. Not now, of course, not today, not even this year. She would wait until Helen's fourteenth birthday perhaps, in June. Paul would be sixteen, nearly seventeen then. They would be well able to decide for themselves what to do. She made herself a cup of coffee and stirred it thoughtfully. The trouble about most people leaving home is that they do it on impulse. She wouldn't do that. She'd give herself plenty of time and do it right. She would find a job first, a good job. It was a pity about RTE, but it was too close. She could get promoted there if she had only herself to think about. But no, of course not, she had to get away. Maybe London, or some other part of Dublin anyway, not on her own doorstep. It would cause too much excitement.

She heard him upstairs brushing his teeth. She knew that he would go out for a drink this morning. There was no way she could be his guard. Suppose he said he wanted to go out and buy something; she could offer to get it for him, but he would think of something that only he himself could do.

There were maybe another thirty or forty years left. She

She sat at the kitchen table and decided she would leave him.

couldn't spend them with her heart all tied up in knots like this. She could not spend those years half-waking, half-sleeping in an armchair, wondering how they would bring him in. And even more frightening was watching and waiting in case he went back to drink, the watching and waiting of the last five months. She would be blamed, of course . . . selfish, heartless, no sense of her duty. How could anyone leave home like that? Emma believed that quite a lot of people could do it, if the situation at home was as bad as hers was.

She heard Gerry come downstairs.

'I brought down the tea things,' he said, like a child expecting to be praised.

'Oh, that's grand, thanks.' She took the things from him. He hadn't touched the grapefruit, nor the tea.

'Look, I'm fine. Why don't you go into work? Seriously, Emma, you'd only be half an hour late.'

'Well, I might, if you're sure . . .'

'No, I'm feeling great now,' he said.

'What are you going to do this morning, start phoning some of the contacts you've written to?'

'Yes, yes.' He was impatient.

'I might go in.' She stood up. His face was pure relief.

'Do. You'd feel better. I know you and your feelings about your job.'

'Listen before I go. There's a job vacant in Paddy's business, only an assistant at the moment, but if you were interested, he said that he'd be delighted for you to come in, for a year or two, until you got yourself sorted out.' She looked at him hopefully.

He looked back restlessly. He didn't know that so much of his future and hers rested on the reply he gave.

'An assistant? An assistant to Paddy, of all people? Jesus, he must be mad to suggest it. He only suggested it so that he could boast about it. I wouldn't touch the job for a million pounds.'

'Right. I just thought you should know.'

'Oh, I'm not saying a word against you. It's that little bastard Paddy.'

'Well, take it easy.'

'You're very good to me, not complaining, not telling me what a complete fool I made of myself, of both of us.'

'There's no point.'

'I won't let you down again. Listen, I have to go into town for a couple of things this morning – is there anything you . . .?'

She shook her head wordlessly and went to the garage to take out her bicycle. She wheeled it to the gate and looked back and waved. It didn't matter that people would blame her. They blamed her already. A man doesn't drink like that unless there's something very wrong with his marriage. In a way, her leaving would create more respect for Gerry. People would say that the poor devil must have had a lot to put up with over the years.

GLOSSARY

alcoholic a person who drinks too much alcohol and who cannot
control their drinking

anonymous with a name that is not known or not made public
(*Alcoholics Anonymous* is a support group for people with
drinking problems)

bastard (*slang*) a worthless or cruel person (usually male)

bedsitter (bedsit) a room used for both living and sleeping in

biscuit a kind of cake or bread, which is small, thin, flat, and hard

bloody a swearword, often used for emphasis (e.g. *bloody awful*)

booze (*informal*) alcoholic drink

Bovril a hot drink made from meat extracts

breadwinner (*informal*) the person whose earnings support
his/her family

career progress and development of one's professional working
life

cereal a kind of breakfast food made from grains (oats, wheat, etc.)

champagne a special white wine that has bubbles in it

chat up (*informal*) to talk in a friendly way to someone of the
opposite sex

commission (*n*) a piece of work that somebody has asked you to
do and will pay you for

concert a musical entertainment given in public

course medical treatment for a certain length of time

cow (*derogatory slang*) the word for a farm animal used as a very
offensive term for a woman

devil (*informal*) a person

eyeshadow colour painted on the eyelids

fellow (*informal*) a man or a boy

flatmate somebody who lives in the same flat as you
Garda an Irish word for a guard (a kind of policeman)
gin a colourless alcoholic drink
give up to stop doing something (often a habit)
grapefruit a fruit like an orange, but yellow, larger and more
    bitter
hangover the unpleasant after-effects of drinking too much
    alcohol
high-class belonging to the upper social classes
hostel a building in which cheap food and lodging are provided
hug (*v*) to put your arms round somebody tightly in a loving way
kid (*informal*) a child or young person
kidnap to take somebody away by violence and keep them hidden
label to write a name on something to show who the owner is
landlord the person who owns a flat which is rented out to other
    people
lemonade a sweet fizzy drink
make-up powder and coloured paints used by women on their
    faces
mascara a kind of make-up used for darkening the eyelashes
master the person (or thing) that has greater power and is in
    control
mess a dirty, untidy, or disorganized state
mug a large cup, usually with straight sides
nun a woman who has taken religious vows and lives in a convent
one-horse town (*informal*) a quiet town without much business or
    entertainment
pill a small round or flat piece of medicine to be swallowed whole
    (*the pill* is used to mean the medicine taken by women to
    prevent pregnancy)
pint a unit of liquid measure, approximately half a litre

print (*n*) a photograph produced from the negative film

punk a young person who wears strange clothes and has brightly coloured hair, like punk rock musicians

rape to commit the crime of forcing someone to have sexual intercourse against their will

ridiculous very silly; deserving to be laughed at

(as) right as rain (*idiom*) in excellent health or working order

saint a very good, unselfish, or patient person

sausage a kind of prepared meat in a thin, tube-like shape

sob to cry noisily and with great emotion

sober with one's actions and thoughts not affected by alcohol

sociable friendly; fond of the company of other people

sort (things/oneself) out (*informal*) to arrange, tidy, or put things in order; to organize oneself, or find solutions to a problem

stage the raised platform or area where a theatrical or musical performance takes place

tonic water mineral water flavoured with quinine

Dublin People
SHORT STORIES

ACTIVITIES

Before Reading

1 In the first story a young country girl comes to live in Dublin. What are the differences for young people between living with one's family and living independently, and between country life and city life? Explain your ideas, using these prompts.

   • family / friends / neighbours
   • social life (parties, discos, clubs, cinemas, theatres, sports)
   • living on one's own (expense, housework, loneliness)
   • working life (job opportunities, wages, transport to work)
   • quality of life (boredom/interest, noise/peacefulness, air/water/food, shopping)

2 Read the story introduction and the back cover. Can you guess what might happen to Jo in this story? Here are some possibilities. Circle Y (Yes) or N (No) for each sentence.

   1 Jo enjoys her new job and is happy in it. Y/N
   2 She leaves her job after a few weeks, can't find another, and runs out of money. Y/N
   3 She goes out nearly every night to parties or dances. Y/N
   4 She lives on her own, makes no new friends, and is miserable, lonely, and homesick. Y/N
   5 She makes some friends, and is happy some of the time. Y/N
   6 After a few months she gives up her job and goes home to her family in the country. Y/N
   7 She falls in love and gets married. Y/N

3 In the second story Gerry Moore has a problem with alcohol, which is also hard for his family. Which of these problems do *you* think would be hardest to live with? Put them in order, 1 to 10 (with 1 for the worst problem).

One member of a family (a partner, parent, sister, etc.) . . .

- can't keep any job for more than a few months.
- is in trouble with the police.
- is in prison.
- spends too much money and is always in debt.
- is always borrowing money and never pays it back.
- is an alcoholic and gets drunk every night.
- has a relationship outside his/her marriage.
- is physically violent towards members of the family.
- has a serious mental illness and is a danger to other people.
- is very ill and needs nursing day and night.

4 Read the story introduction and the back cover again. How would you *like* Gerry's story to end? Choose one of these possible endings and explain why you would prefer it.

1 Gerry loses his battle with alcohol, can't keep a job, and his life gets worse and worse.

2 He wins the battle, never touches another drop of alcohol, and is a miserable man for the rest of his life.

3 He neither wins nor loses, and life for him and his family goes on as it did before.

4 Something terrible happens (Gerry dies or kills himself; he kills his wife or one of his children in a drunken rage; someone kills him).

While Reading

Read the first story, *Flat in Ringsend*, up to the bottom of page 39, and then answer these questions.

1 Describe Jo's family back at home.
2 How were Jo's dreams of life in Dublin different from the reality?
3 Why was Jo surprised when she first met Pauline?
4 What did Jo realize on Thursday night when she took a phone message for one of the nurses?
5 How did Jo get to know Gerry and Christy?
6 How did the scene in the kitchen show the difference between Jo's character and Nessa's and Pauline's?
7 Why was Jo so worried by Friday night?
8 How did the party in the nurses' flat come to an end?

Before you read the rest of *Flat in Ringsend* (page 40 to the end), can you guess how the story will end? Choose one of these possibilities.

1 Jo tells the guards about her fears for Nessa and Pauline. They take her down to the Garda station, question her, and the next day start a search for the missing girls.
2 Jo tells the guards her fears, but they just laugh at her and tell her not to be so silly.
3 Jo says nothing to the guards, spends a miserable night, and on Sunday Nessa and Pauline return home. Jo never tells them how anxious she had been.

Read the second story, *Murmurs in Montrose*, up to the bottom of page 80. Who said or thought this, and who were they talking to, or thinking about?

1 'Because he's often here when there's a crisis, isn't he?'
2 'You're fine, there's nothing the matter with you, you can have a drink as well as the next man.'
3 He sounded grand. Please, please, God, let it be all right.
4 Maybe his mind had gone to pieces in that place, talking all this emotional rubbish, and tears in his eyes.
5 'Don't think yours is the only [home] where people shout at each other, you know.'
6 'Is he listening to you, there in the room?'
7 'I've missed you, old son, I really have.'

Before you read the rest of *Murmurs in Montrose*, (page 81 to the end), what do you think Gerry should do at this point?

1 He should continue sorting out his study and looking for new photographic work in Dublin.
2 He should leave Ireland and start again in a new country, or look for a different kind of job.
3 He should phone Des Kelly back and cancel their next day's meeting in a pub.

Now read the story to the end and answer these questions.

1 What do you think was the turning point for Gerry in his battle against alcohol?
2 What do you think was the turning point for Emma in her decision to leave Gerry?

ACTIVITIES

After Reading

1 **Put this summary of the last part of *Flat in Ringsend* in the right order. Then, using these linking words, join the parts together to make a paragraph of five sentences.**

and / and after that / and in the end / because / but / so / then / when

(3) 1 ___so___ she went down to the party in the nurses' flat
(7) 2 the guards were called
(12) 3 _and in the end_ persuaded her that she was being silly
(1) 4 by Saturday night there was still no sign of Nessa and Pauline
(8) 5 _and_ the party came to an end
(9) 6 _and after that_ Jo fainted on the stairs
(5) 7 _because_ Jo really believed that they had been kidnapped
(10) 8 the guards carried her upstairs to her flat
(2) 9 at midnight she was still wide awake
(4) 10 _but_ she didn't enjoy it at all
(6) 11 _then_ somebody threw a stone through the window
(11) 12 _and_ they sat and talked with her over a cup of tea

2 **On Sunday Mickey writes a letter home to his mother. Use the notes he made in his guard's notebook to write the letter for him.**

Saturday night. Disturbance at flat in Ringsend (me and Sean). Broken window, uninvited guests, no real problem. Girl from upstairs flat fainted. Carried her up. Tea. Country girl – some very silly ideas (kidnapping, murder, etc.)! Nice girl, though. Monday evening, 8 o'clock.

3 **Imagine that on Sunday evening Nessa and Pauline come home and find Jo in the kitchen. Complete their conversation.**

NESSA: Hallo, Jo. Had a good weekend?

JO: _____

PAULINE: What's all this about? What are you crying for?

JO: _____

NESSA: Worried? Why on earth were you worried about us?

JO: _____

NESSA: But we often go away for the weekend.

PAULINE: Yeah, if there's a good party somewhere, we just go.

JO: _____

PAULINE: Why should we tell you?

NESSA: Anyway, why were you worried about us?

JO: _____

PAULINE: What drunk men? What are you talking about?

JO: _____

NESSA: Apologize? What for?

JO: _____

NESSA: Go on, what did you think? You've got to tell us now.

JO: _____

PAULINE: You thought WHAT! Oh, my God, did you hear that, Pauline? That's so funny!

NESSA: Don't laugh at poor Jo, Pauline. It was kind of her to be concerned, even if it was a bit silly.

JO: _____

PAULINE: Mickey? Who's Mickey?

NESSA: Jo – you've gone all pink in the face!

4 Jack Moore, in *Murmurs in Montrose*, worries about his brother and Emma. Here are his thoughts on the way to work one morning. Choose one suitable word to fill each gap.

I don't know what's going on _____ Emma and Gerry. Emma looks very _____ and worried, and who can blame _____? Gerry's been out for four months _____, and what's he been doing all _____ time? I know he hasn't started _____ again – well, he says he hasn't – _____ when is he going to get _____ work? Mother says that Gerry needs _____ rest, but I'm afraid Mother just _____ understand the problem. Poor Emma! She's a _____ she really is. She's wonderful, the _____ she manages Gerry and is so _____ and never complains. I hope he _____ her, but I don't think he _____. Emma said she and Gerry were _____ to a wedding in September, but _____ don't think they should go. There's _____ to be alcohol at a wedding. _____ says she must trust Gerry, and _____ must make his own decisions, take _____ of his own life, but I _____ know . . .

5 The phrasal verbs below are all used in the story *Murmurs in Montrose*. Choose the best verb to make sentences using these notes. Use a dictionary to help you if necessary.

hang up / call in / break down / be fed up with / go on / give up / bring up / let somebody down / sort out / put up with / build up

1 Gerry's mother // five boys on her own.
2 Gerry told his mother his health // from all the long working hours.
3 Everybody wondered if Gerry Moore had a strong enough character // drinking.
4 After the wedding Gerry promised Emma never // again.

112

5 When Jack phoned and talked on and on, Emma knew that if she // she would feel guilty.

6 On Gerry's first night home, Helen asked Father Vincent if he // on some excuse.

7 Gerry spent a long time // his study.

8 Emma doubted that Gerry would be able // his business again.

9 The debts were growing and Emma wondered how long it // .

10 Gerry's mother // Emma's clever talk and long medical words.

11 Paul and Helen thought that their parents being emotional was as bad as having to // their father's drinking.

6 **Which of these statements about *Murmurs in Montrose* do you agree with (A), and which do you disagree with (D)? If you disagree, say why.**

1 Emma should have thrown away all the alcohol in the house before Gerry came home from the nursing home.

2 Gerry tried hard to change his habits and his way of life.

3 At the end of the story Gerry seems to be losing his battle and will probably soon become an alcoholic again.

4 If Emma had been more sympathetic, Gerry might have found his battle easier.

5 Gerry's mother and Des Kelly helped Gerry a lot.

6 Emma was selfish and heartless to decide to leave Gerry in a couple of years' time.

7 Gerry was his own worst enemy.

7 The people in Maeve Binchy's stories are very true to life, with problems and worries just like the rest of us. Here are six letters to a 'problem page' in a magazine. Which characters from the two stories wrote these letters? Then choose two letters and write a letter of advice in reply to each.

1 A girl I work with at the post office has a wonderful life. She lives on her own in a flat and can go out at night to parties and pubs and wherever she wants. I want to have an independent life too, but my parents won't let me leave home. What can I do?

Envious

2 I'm nearly seventeen. My dad is drunk most of the time and my mum can't bear it any more. She's going to live in London and wants me to go with her. My dad wants me to stay with him. My friend Andy's parents say I can go and live with them. I don't know what to do.

Undecided

3 My sister has gone to live on her own in the big city, but she's very young and we all know she can't manage by herself. I think she should come home at once, but she's being stupid and just won't listen to me. How can I persuade her?

Angry and worried

4 A friend of mine seems very depressed. We used to have a grand time together, going out drinking in pubs, but now he says he's giving up alcohol and can't go to pubs. I tell him one little drink now and then would cheer him up, but he still won't come. How can I get him to enjoy life again?

Concerned Friend

114

5 A month ago I left my husband. He is an alcoholic and our life had become unbearable. His mother has just written to tell me I am selfish and have ruined my husband's life. I feel terrible. Is she right? Should I have stayed with my husband?
  Guilty

6 One of the girls in the flat upstairs is always coming down to our flat for cups of tea. She says she's lonely and homesick and wants someone to talk to. My flatmates and I don't want to be unkind, but we all have our own social lives and the girl is becoming a bit of a bore. What should we say to her?
  Annoyed

8 **Both stories have 'open' endings. In your opinion, which of these developments does the author lead us to expect?**

1 Nessa and Pauline return on Sunday. Jo goes out with Mickey on Monday and starts to enjoy life in Dublin.

2 The girls do not return, and have in fact been kidnapped or murdered by Gerry and Christy. Jo never forgives herself.

3 Gerry goes to Paddy's that morning and gets the assistant's job. He never drinks again and Emma stays with him.

4 Gerry Moore goes out for a drink that morning and falls back into his old, bad habits. Emma leaves him two years later.

ABOUT THE AUTHOR

Maeve Binchy was born in 1940 in Dublin. After school and university in Ireland she became a teacher in various girls' schools, and wrote travel articles in the long summer holidays. In 1969 she joined the *Irish Times* as a journalist. She is now based in London and travels all over the world writing articles from many different places.

She has written plays for the stage and for television, and is the author of many bestsellers, both novels and volumes of short stories. Among her novels are *Light a Penny Candle*, *Firefly Summer*, *The Copper Beech*, *The Glass Lake*, and *Tara Road*. Her novel *Circle of Friends* was made into a film in 1995. Her short-story collections include *Central Line*, *Victoria Line* and *The Lilac Bus*, which is a set of linked short stories about the passengers who travel regularly on a small country bus. The two stories retold in this book are from her collection entitled *Dublin 4* (Ringsend and Montrose are districts in the city of Dublin).

Maeve Binchy's books are affectionate pictures of the lives of ordinary people, often in small Irish towns in the earlier years of this century. Important events tend to happen offstage, and her stories concentrate on birth, friendship, marriage, death, and the small details of everyday life. She makes gentle fun of her characters, turning village gossip into art, and leaves us with a strong sense of the confusion of life, full of joys and sadnesses at the same time.

ABOUT BOOKWORMS

OXFORD BOOKWORMS LIBRARY
Classics • True Stories • Fantasy & Horror • Human Interest
Crime & Mystery • Thriller & Adventure

The OXFORD BOOKWORMS LIBRARY offers a wide range of original and adapted stories, both classic and modern, which take learners from elementary to advanced level through six carefully graded language stages:

Stage 1 (400 headwords)	**Stage 4** (1400 headwords)
Stage 2 (700 headwords)	**Stage 5** (1800 headwords)
Stage 3 (1000 headwords)	**Stage 6** (2500 headwords)

More than fifty titles are also available on cassette, and there are many titles at Stages 1 to 4 which are specially recommended for younger learners. In addition to the introductions and activities in each Bookworm, resource material includes photocopiable test worksheets and Teacher's Handbooks, which contain advice on running a class library and using cassettes, and the answers for the activities in the books.

Several other series are linked to the OXFORD BOOKWORMS LIBRARY. They range from highly illustrated readers for young learners, to playscripts, non-fiction readers, and unsimplified texts for advanced learners.

Oxford Bookworms Starters   *Oxford Bookworms Factfiles*
Oxford Bookworms Playscripts   *Oxford Bookworms Collection*

Details of these series and a full list of all titles in the OXFORD BOOKWORMS LIBRARY can be found in the *Oxford English* catalogues. A selection of titles from the OXFORD BOOKWORMS LIBRARY can be found on the next pages.

Jane Eyre

CHARLOTTE BRONTË

Retold by Clare West

Jane Eyre is alone in the world. Disliked by her aunt's family, she is sent away to school. Here she learns that a young girl, with neither money nor family to support her, can expect little from the world. She survives, but she wants more from life than simply to survive: she wants respect, and love. When she goes to work for Mr Rochester, she hopes she has found both at once. But the sound of strange laughter, late at night, behind a locked door, warns her that her troubles are only beginning.

Pride and Prejudice

JANE AUSTEN

Retold by Clare West

'The moment I first met you, I noticed your pride, your sense of superiority, and your selfish disdain for the feelings of others. You are the last man in the world whom I could ever be persuaded to marry,' said Elizabeth Bennet.

And so Elizabeth rejects the proud Mr Darcy. Can nothing overcome her prejudice against him? And what of the other Bennet girls – their fortunes, and misfortunes, in the business of getting husbands?

This famous novel by Jane Austen is full of wise and humorous observation of the people and manners of her times.

Decline and Fall

EVELYN WAUGH

Retold by Clare West

After a wild, drunken party, Paul Pennyfeather is forced to leave Oxford and begin a new life out in the wide world. His experiences take him from a boys' private school in Wales, where he meets some rather strange people, to a life of luxury in a grand country house and the Ritz Hotel, and then to seven years' hard labour in prison. Where will it all end?

The black humour of this story about English society in the 1920s is as fresh today as it was when the novel was first written.

Cold Comfort Farm

STELLA GIBBONS

Retold by Clare West

The farm lies in the shadow of a hill, and the farmyard rarely sees the sun, even in summer, when the sukebind hangs heavy in the branches. Here live the Starkadders – Aunt Ada Doom, Judith, Amos, Seth, Reuben, Elfine . . . They lead messy, untidy lives, full of dark thoughts, moody silences, and sudden noisy quarrels.

That is, until their attractive young cousin arrives from London. Neat, sensible, efficient, Flora Poste cannot *bear* messes (they are so *uncivilized*). She begins to tidy up the Starkadders' lives at once . . .

OXFORD BOOKWORMS COLLECTION
Fiction by well-known authors, both classic and modern.
Texts are not abridged or simplified in any way, but have
notes and questions to help the reader.

From the Cradle to the Grave
Short stories by
EVELYN WAUGH, SOMERSET MAUGHAM, ROALD DAHL, SAKI,
FRANK SARGESON, RAYMOND CARVER, H. E. BATES, SUSAN HILL

This collection of short stories explores the trials of life from youth to old age: the idealism of young people, the stresses of marriage, the anxieties of parenthood, and the loneliness and fears of older people. There is a wide variety of styles of writing, from black humour and satire to compassionate and realistic observation of the follies and foibles of humankind.

A Window on the Universe
Short stories by
RAY BRADBURY, BILL BROWN, PHILIP K. DICK,
ARTHUR C. CLARKE, JEROME BIXBY, ISAAC ASIMOV, BRIAN ALDISS,
JOHN WYNDHAM, ROALD DAHL

What does the future hold in store for the human race? Aliens from distant galaxies, telepathic horror, interstellar war, time-warps, the shriek of a rose, collision with an asteroid – the unknown lies around every corner, and the universe is a big place. These nine science-fiction stories offer possibilities that are fantastic, humorous, alarming, but always thought-provoking.